HONEYMOON HUSBAND

Other books by Shirley Marks:

Geek to Chic

HONEYMOON HUSBAND

•

Shirley Marks

AVALON BOOKS
NEW YORK

Published by Thomas Bouregy & Co., Inc.
160 Madison Avenue, New York, NY 10016

Library of Congress Cataloging-in-Publication Data

Marks, Shirley.
  Honeymoon husband / Shirley Marks.
        p. cm.
  ISBN 978-0-8034-9852-5 (acid-free paper)
  I. Title.

PS3613.A7655H66 2007
813'.6—dc22

                                                    2007016628

PRINTED IN THE UNITED STATES OF AMERICA
ON ACID-FREE PAPER
BY HADDON CRAFTSMEN, BLOOMSBURG, PENNSYLVANIA

To the multi-talented Cindy A.
Is there nothing you can't do?

You came up with the title and encouraged me
to write the story.

I miss your unique observations, upbeat
outlook on life, and infectious laughter.

To my darling husband, your love and humor
mean more to me than you can possibly know.
May our honeymoon continue!

Chapter One

I *can't marry you*, Earl had scrawled on the waxy inside of a hamburger wrapper. Hannah Roberts must have read it at least a hundred times. She crumbled it into a ball and then smoothed the wrapper out again and read it a hundred more.

Why couldn't he have told her sooner? How about last week or yesterday or even fifteen minutes before she boarded the plane for Maui?

They'd flown from Wichita, Kansas to Phoenix, Arizona for three hours. And he still had the seat right next to her for the next two-hour trip from Phoenix, Arizona to Los Angeles, California.

Plenty of time to talk, you would think. But that's not what happened. Earl hadn't said a word.

The last time she'd seen him was only minutes

1

before boarding their connecting flight for the last leg of their journey, he was running back to pick up a snack.

"I'll catch up with you," is what he said.

Famous last words.

The instant the landing gear made contact with the runway of the Waikalua Airport she jolted in her seat—partly because airplane landings were new to her and partly because this was the biggest moment in her life.

She was *alone*.

There wasn't going to be a wedding and on what was supposed to be her honeymoon—she was *alone*.

"Please stay seated until the plane has come to a full and complete stop at the gate," an airline attendant's voice crackled over the loudspeaker. "The captain will turn off the fasten seatbelt sign when it is safe for you to move about the cabin and disembark."

Excitement built within the cabin of the 757. People whispered and shifted in their seats. Everyone was anxious to step onto Hawaiian soil. Everyone except Hannah.

Maybe she could just stay in her seat. Maybe they wouldn't notice an extra passenger and she could fly back home.

"Excuse me, Miss." A male flight attendant

touched Hannah on the shoulder. "You can de-plane now. Enjoy your stay in Maui."

Enjoy? Hannah turned in her seat and stared at him. A honeymoon without a husband didn't sound like a good time.

She folded her *Dear Jane* letter and slipped it into her purse. By the time she looked up, the plane was nearly empty. The last of the passengers stood in the aisles toward the front of the plane on their way out.

The knot in her stomach tightened and the doubt in her mind strengthened but there was nothing she could do about it. What choice did she really have?

Hannah unfastened her seatbelt and stood. She retrieved her carry-on from the overhead bin and headed to the terminal.

Even though Maui, Hawaii was only a different state, it felt like a different country. One man after another passed her wearing colorful Aloha shirts, ranging from bright splashes of orange, red, and yellow to more subdued tones of blue, green, and brown. Women, both scorched and tanned, wore similar tropical prints, and everyone really did wear flower leis.

Hannah gripped the handle of her carry-on and swallowed hard. She really was alone. Far from home and in a strange land.

"Hannah! Hannah!" someone, a woman called out. The voice sounded familiar. "Over here!"

Hannah couldn't imagine who would be calling her, not here. She stood on tiptoe, scanning over the top of the crowd. She spied a frantically waving hand and blonde hair. Christine?

The last place Hannah expected to see her best friend was in the middle of a crowded airport two time zones away from home. Only yesterday Hannah had been Christine's bridesmaid.

"Aloha! I'm so glad to see you." Christine wrapped her arms around Hannah for a gigantic hug.

"What on earth are you doing here? I mean—at the airport? You're supposed to be on your honeymoon." According to Hannah, Christine got one of the best, maybe the last, of the good men on Earth.

"And you're on yours, right? Well, almost." Christine returned, teasing. "Tim and I have a whole wonderful week here together. We wanted to make sure you two were okay."

We. Hannah gulped. To be half of a *we* sounded nice—she might never be part of a *we*.

"Our arrival times were only a half hour different from yours so we decided that by the time we waited for the luggage and got the rental car, you two would have landed and then we could all leave together and we could give you a lift because we'll drive right by your hotel on the way to ours."

Ours. Hannah sighed. Something that two people claim together—would she ever share anything with another person?

"You don't have to do that." Two newlywed couples hanging around was one thing—almost cute, but it wasn't going to happen with Earl gone. The last thing she wanted to do was to be Christine and Tim's pathetic third wheel.

"I can't believe you won a two-week, all-expense-paid honeymoon!" Christine bubbled with a fresh bout of enthusiasm. "You're so lucky." She glanced around, finally looking down the jetway. "Where is Earl, anyway?"

"He's not here." Hannah wasn't looking forward to breaking the news to her friend. "You really should be with Tim."

"What do you mean, Earl's not here? I thought it was all planned. You two are supposed to be getting married. What happened?"

"Well, he only came halfway with me, and I don't think we'll be getting married anymore." Hannah really couldn't say, Earl hadn't gone into detail. He didn't have to. His note said it all.

"Halfway? You mean he's abandoned you?"

Yeah, that was true. He left her. But did Christine have to say it like that?

"Oh, my gosh. You poor thing. Oh, Hannah, are you all right?" Tears filled Christine's eyes and she wrapped her arm around Hannah, comforting her.

Then Hannah started to tear up. She didn't want to cry in front of strangers and especially not in front of Christine.

"I'll be fine, really." Hannah did her best to put on a brave smile, but Christine would probably see through it. She always had.

"Earl's strung you along for the last five years, but I never expected him to do this. I never thought he was good enough for you. What a jerk!"

Hannah didn't think he was a jerk, exactly, but he certainly had let her down. After all, he'd proposed after they graduated high school and she expected they would marry soon after.

Christine was far more upset about it than Hannah was. Hannah felt too numb to be angry.

"Come on." Christine stepped forward, still with her arm around Hannah. "Let's go. We'll meet Tim in front of baggage claim."

Christine led Hannah by the arm into the stream of people walking through the terminal. They waited next to the luggage carousel and watched the luggage from flight 247 roll by on the conveyer belt.

Big ones, small ones, black ones, burgundy ones, and then her two brown soft-sided pieces popped up over the opening and slid onto the main conveyer belt. For easy identification, she'd tied a yellow pom-pom on her bag and a green one on his.

"That's it, just these," Hannah announced. The two huge pieces of luggage were also part of the contest prize. Except that Earl wouldn't need his vacation clothes.

He had promised he'd marry her once they'd arrived and they were supposed to enjoy the honeymoon she'd won together. But it wasn't going to happen.

Why had he left? Was it something Hannah had done? Something she hadn't done? She didn't know, but it must have been her fault.

With luggage in hand, she and Christine left baggage claim and headed outside. Hannah passed through the automatic doors of the terminal and the balmy air blew against her.

Balmy, not hot.

Around her palm trees swayed, lush, green vegetation sprang out from every surface, every crevice. The Hawaiian Islands was just as she had always heard about and imagined . . . paradise.

A new white rental sedan came to a stop at the curb in front of them. Out popped Christine's new husband Tim from the driver's side.

"Hello, Chrissie-kins." Tim leaned toward her to capture a precious kiss.

"Hi, sweetie." Christine met him halfway and planted a big one square on his lips. They gazed at one another with what Hannah could only describe as a couple totally, completely in love.

Hannah sighed, wishing someone would look at her like that. Earl certainly didn't, never had.

"Nice to see you, Hannah. Where's Earl?" Tim took a quick glance around. But there was nothing wrong with his eyesight, Earl wasn't here.

"I'll tell you about it later, honey."

"Oh." Tim took her word for it and moved on. "Isn't Maui wonderful, Hannah?"

"Beautiful. Warm," she returned with not much enthusiasm and put on the best cheery smile she could.

"Here, let me take that for you." Tim pulled their two small bags out of the trunk and placed Hannah's two larger-sized pieces in first.

How embarrassing for her. Hannah might not have brought a husband but she sure had enough clothes to dress one.

Nearly an hour later, Hannah waved goodbye to Christine and Tim as they drove away from the Neilani Resort. She tried not to stare with her mouth open and look like the country girl who'd never seen the big city, but she couldn't help it. She had seen the big city, but she never seen anything like this hotel.

What they called the lobby didn't look like the kind of lobby of any hotel she'd seen before, ever. She followed the marbled-floor through the hotel's large glass front doors right into the six-floor-high indoor garden. In the center of the pavilion sat a huge open air bar, surrounding it a long, wide pond, almost big enough for an Olympic poolside event.

"May I help you?" A hotel employee, standing behind the front desk, beckoned Hannah closer.

Did she look that lost?

"I'm . . . I want to check in."

"Do you have a reservation?"

"Yes, I—" She rummaged through her purse, feeling for the envelope, those honeymoon contest papers were there somewhere. "Here."

"Ah, yes." The man glanced at the letter and smiled wide. "Mr. and Mrs. Henderson. The winners of this year's Heavenly Hawaiian Honeymoon Contest."

He looked up at her and she stared back. Why did he have to look at her like that? Did he know? Could he tell that she'd shown up without a husband?

"Congratulations." By the way the desk employee's gaze darted around, Hannah was sure he was looking for Earl. "Is Mr. Henderson—"

"He's not here—" She started to explain and didn't know where to begin. "He's—"

"That's fine." The clerk turned back to his desk and handed a pen to her. "If you would sign-in, please."

Hannah signed where he indicated.

"And here are your room keys. You'll be staying in the honeymoon suite in the main building. Just let us know when Mr. Henderson returns and we'll be happy to show you to your suite."

What she'd meant was that Mr. Henderson wasn't here—period.

"The Wailea Neilani wishes you and your husband a happy stay in Maui," the desk clerk continued. "If there is anything we can do for you, please don't hesitate to ask."

Hannah took the room key cards, held onto one and slipped the extra key into her purse. Turning away from the front desk, she caught sight of plants growing from the second floor, hanging overhead.

How did they get plants to grow from—her question was cut short when she slammed into something. Hannah pitched forward and all she could see was the water in the pond coming up fast to meet her.

Jeremy Gordon didn't have time to yell out a warning. He caught the woman with the honey blond hair before she took a header and set her square on her feet. "Are you okay?"

"What?" She stared up at him, her eyes unfocused.

"I don't think the koi will be too thrilled about you joining them, and I didn't think you wanted to go swimming without your swimsuit."

She didn't say a word. She looked down, checking her clothes. When she gazed up at him, his world polar-shifted. One moment he was right side up and in an instant it flipped upside down.

She, whoever she was, had the most amazing eyes. They were a beautiful blue. But not sky blue and not deep blue of the ocean, but the warm, welcoming green-blue found only in tropical waters.

"I'm sorry." She straightened. "I wasn't watching where I was going."

"No, problem." With an armful of newly-arrived-mainlander, Jeremy made sure she was steady before releasing her and stepping back. He didn't want her going over again and getting hurt.

"Eh, *brah, howzit?*" the familiar voice, a Hawaiian local interrupted.

"Luka? What are you doing here?" Jeremy almost didn't recognize him without a cab.

When Jeremy had first arrived, a couple of months ago, it seemed no matter what cab he got in, no matter what island he was on, Luka sat behind the wheel.

"Working . . . *mo bettah* than *drivin da* cab." He wore the sedate patterned Aloha shirt and shorts of the Neilani employees. "I *tink* you on the Big Island, no?"

"Yeah, but I'll be here for the next week." Jeremy glanced over at the woman, still concerned about her.

"Your girl?"

"No, I bumped into her. Actually, she ran into me. Do you think you can see her to her room?"

"*K'den.*" Luka smiled when he looked at the woman, seeming more than anxious to do his job.

Jeremy scooped the plastic card she'd dropped off the ground and looked her in the eyes. "Luka works here . . . you can just follow him. He'll show you to your room."

"Okay," she said, sounding stronger.

Jeremy was still slightly concerned that she'd rattled her coconut. "Are you going to be all right?" He looked at her, trying to decide if she was okay, but he couldn't help but get lost in her eyes again. Then he noticed that she had the most adorable nose.

"Fine. Thank you," she said, but Jeremy didn't completely buy it.

"Here's her key." He handed the plastic card to Luka. "Remember . . . she's a guest."

"See ya round, *brah,* yeah?" Luka waved.

"Okay, later." Jeremy hesitated. He knew the woman would be all right, but he hated leaving her. She still looked a bit dazed.

A minute later she and Luka were out of sight, and Jeremy headed over to the front desk to check in.

Crazy lady. Under different circumstances maybe he would . . . maybe. . . .

No, Jeremy wasn't here for a good time. He didn't

think he'd have to remind himself but then again, he thought about those eyes and her whole neat package, she'd sure make a fine week's distraction.

"Room 114, sir." The hotel clerk handed over the key. "Would you like someone to take you to your room?"

Jeremy had been in enough hotels to find his way around any of them by himself. "No, thanks. Just point me in the right direction."

The clerk slid out a layout of the hotel across the desk and circled the lobby then drew a line around the Makai tower and past the Kukui tower to his final destination. "Your room is located here—on the ground floor."

Jeremy trekked through the lobby and around the four-poster bar that sat in its center. Ten minutes later he stood inside his room. It looked like any other hotel room—bathroom, bedroom table, two chairs, desk, dresser, TV hidden in the cabinet, and bed.

He stepped to the window to admire his view. Hawaiian tropical foliage—ground floor, what did he expect? The Ali'i suite with a view of Haleakala or Molokini? Nope, he was here to do a job and nothing more—they had given him a place to sleep and that's all he needed.

Jeremy dug out the envelope he'd been given containing his instructions. On the outside Russell had written—*Jerry*.

He didn't like being called Jerry.

As he opened the envelope it just occurred to him that he might have to dress the part and hoped that he didn't have to wear one of those touristy shirts. Aloha shirt—he hated those shirts that vacationers snatched up and hauled home by the dozens.

The letter said that he could wear some generic astronomy tees—planets, various galaxies and star clusters, something a regular person could recognize. It wouldn't kill Jeremy to wear a shirt with a picture of Saturn or a spiral galaxy.

He hated wasting his time here, nothing to do, nothing to accomplish. It was his dad and brother who made the headlines while Jeremy had played around at sports, at parties, and with women.

He didn't have the typical life of most astronomers. He'd climbed the Himalayas, biked through Europe, and even downhill-skied the pro circuit. He'd spent so much time on the road, he didn't even have a place he called home.

Jeremy had wasted his life *playing*. His father let him and his older brother, Robert, pursue whatever had interested them. They both chose to follow their father with a doctorate in astrophysics, but it was Robert who had followed their dad into the observatory while Jeremy beat a path as far away as he could.

It had been a huge mistake and Jeremy was going to do his best to make up for those young, wasted years. He wanted his chance to prove he wasn't the no-talent that his family thought he was, but he wasn't going to prove anything to anyone playing guide to the stars for a bunch of tourists.

"How could you miss them? How?" Lance Dumont of Heavenly Hawaiian Honeymoons moved the phone receiver from one ear to the other. "Weren't they on the plane?" He opened the Henderson file on his desk, not believing his bad luck.

"Airline says yes, but I didn't see them and I don't know where they went." The company limo driver didn't sound half as concerned as Lance felt. "I was at the right gate, I held up their sign, Henderson, right?"

"Yeah, that's right." Lance checked the Honeymoon Contest contract, verifying the winner's name. "Earl and Hannah Henderson."

"They never showed."

This had never happened before. "I'll check the hotel, maybe they're already there. I'll get back to you." Lance hung up the receiver.

He didn't want to come across as desperate, but he was. Lance needed this to work. The company needed the publicity. He thought giving away a free honeymoon would be so easy—hold the contest, pick the winners, fly them to Maui, get the story, and take their picture for the upcoming bridal magazine.

How hard could that be? Harder than Lance would have ever thought because the honeymoon couple were gone.

Hannah watched Luka swipe the credit-card-looking thing through a device on the door. After it bleeped, a green light flashed before he walked in, followed by Hannah.

He crossed the room to the lanai doors on the far side and pulled them open wide, letting the warm, moist island air in. "Here—see three of the five hotel swimming pools. Over here." He walked to the doors on the adjacent wall and opened them. "*Da* island of Kahoolawe and Molokini."

"Beautiful." Hannah still couldn't get more than a word or two out at a time.

Luka headed back to the door. "*Yo* luggage be here soon."

"Thank you."

He stood there, waiting by the door. For what Hannah wasn't—

"Oh." Hannah popped open her purse to fish for a tip and he held up his hands.

"No, *eviding* taking care of. You make house, Alo-HA." With a nod and friendly smile, he left, pulling the door closed in her room.

This wasn't the way Hannah thought her honeymoon would start. But for now she was glad she was alone. She couldn't face her best friend and loving husband right now. Hannah couldn't stand to see how happy they were—especially compared to how miserable she felt.

Hannah wondered if she would have ever been that happy. She turned back to her room and took a good, long look at the breathtaking views. She and Earl had looked forward to the warm Hawaiian weather, away from the snow blanketed November of Kansas. But she and Earl weren't going to happen.

On the table next to the champagne bottle were two empty flutes, a huge basket of tropical fruit, and an exotic flower arrangement. It was only to be expected. This was, after all, supposed to be a room for a honeymoon couple.

Hannah looked at the card on the table next to the glasses and flowers.

With our compliments, Heavenly Hawaiian Honeymoons.

Tied to the fruit basket handle was another card:

Enjoy your stay with us . . . Wailea Neilani Resort.

Guilt was kicking in. She would have to explain everything, of course. Hannah wasn't a newlywed and she certainly couldn't pretend to be.

Hannah would call the contest people and tell

them that Earl had left her and that she couldn't accept the honeymoon prizes. Of course, she'd have to pay for her flight and then switch to a smaller, less expensive room.

Hannah dug for the contest letter in her purse and skimmed the letterhead for their number. She dialed and after three rings the automated message on the line said:

"Thank you for calling Heavenly Hawaiian Honeymoons. We're open from Monday to Friday from nine AM to five PM. Mahalo."

She hung up the phone. They were closed and she had to wait until tomorrow.

The phone rang and she jumped.

Hannah picked up the receiver immediately. "Hello?"

"Mrs. Henderson?" a man's voice said.

"I think you have the wrong—"

"I'm sorry, I didn't realize you were still using your maiden name."

Maiden name . . . the only reason someone would say maiden name is if they thought you had a *married* name too. Except Hannah didn't have a married name, but this guy didn't know that.

"I'm sorry, this is Lance Dumont from Heavenly Hawaiian Honeymoons, the sponsor of the contest you won. I'm not catching you at a bad time, am I?"

"No, no. It's not a bad time." Hannah glanced

around with the oddest feeling someone was watching her. It was giving her the creeps.

"Good. It seems the limo driver we sent to greet you at the airport missed you and your husband."

What an airhead—Hannah squeezed her eyes shut. *How could she have forgotten about the limo that was supposed to meet her?* "Oh, I'm sorry. I bumped into some friends and they ended up giving me a ride to the hotel."

"It's not a problem. We wanted to greet you personally and set up a convenient time for an interview and snap pictures for the magazine article."

Hannah's adrenaline started pumping and her heart pounded. *Magazine article? There'd be no interview or pictures because there was no Earl.*

"You don't mind if I stop by, do you?"

"Yes, I mean, no, that's fine. Please come by." Hannah's voice was strained, but it wasn't fine, not at all fine. She was a bit nervous about telling this guy about Earl leaving her and she wanted to clear up this mess. That's what was really important. "There's a problem—"

"Not to worry, I'll take care of it when I see you." Then he hung up.

Hannah replaced the phone receiver, wondering, worrying what Lance Dumont was going to do when he found out she didn't have a husband.

Chapter Two

A knock sounded at the door.

Not Lance Dumont already. It just couldn't be. Hannah hadn't even had time to panic, she had just hung up the phone. There wasn't time for anything.

Somehow Hannah made it to the door and with growing uneasiness opened it. She couldn't have been more frightened if Godzilla stood on the other side, but instead of the fire-breathing monster, she was pleasantly surprised to find a hotel employee in his Aloha shirt with his brass luggage trolley.

Relief washed over her. She was saved.

"Where would you like me to put your luggage?" He gestured to the trolley.

21

Hannah pulled the door open. Was she glad to see him. Not so much glad to see *him* as she was glad he wasn't the contest guy. She pointed toward the sofa. "You can leave them right there."

The bellboy set her luggage inside. Without waiting for a tip, he uttered an "Aloha" and left.

What a nice guy. What a nice place. Hannah breathed a bit easier. Even under these horrible circumstances maybe coming here wasn't such a bad idea and she felt optimistic that everything would work out. Hannah could use some time off work, time to herself to get over Earl.

As she closed the door, the nice hotel employee who had brought up her luggage said, "Excuse me, sir."

A second later another knock sounded on her door, and all those freeing thoughts and relaxing feelings evaporated. Dreading who was on the other side of it this time, Hannah turned the handle again. The door felt one hundred times heavier than it had a few minutes ago and it took all her strength to pull it open this time.

"Hello," the man wearing a soft gray and green colored Aloha shirt said from the other side of the door. "I mean . . . Alo-HA. I'm Lance Dumont with Hawaiian Honeymoon Holidays. You must be Hannah Henderson. It's nice to finally meet you."

Oh, no. It *was* him. The contest guy.

She shook his hand with her sweaty one. "It's

nice to meet you too." Hannah wasn't as ready as she thought to confess everything.

"I know you've just arrived and I don't want to bother you two newlyweds, but since our driver missed you at the airport I thought it best to stop by and congratulate you on your recent marriage and for winning the Heavenly Hawaiian Honeymoon Contest."

He looked like a kind, reasonable, understanding person. Hannah hoped he was, anyway. "Ah, yes . . . about the contest. . . ." She had to tell him, explain.

"Is Mr. Henderson around?"

Earl . . . he was talking about Earl.

"I see that he's not here. Out checking jogging routes? Jogging is very popular around here. They have some fantastic trails."

"There's something—"

"That's okay, we spoke only a minute ago, and I'm sure you didn't expect to see me so soon. I called from the lobby, downstairs. It's too bad I missed him. I was hoping to meet the both of you today and to schedule our interview."

She had agreed to it once upon a time when she thought she and Earl would be happily married. Hannah forced her best smile and tried to stay calm.

"We can make it a few days from now, when it's convenient for the two of you. Don't worry about it, we'll set it up later. Let's give you some time to settle in."

"But—" She had to explain, tell him the truth.

"I don't want to take up anymore of your time. I'll be going now."

"But—"

"No, really . . . this can all wait. We'll talk again in a few days."

He wasn't going to give her a chance to explain but she had to—she still had to try.

"I'll bring a photographer to snap some pictures too."

"But—" Hannah had to make him listen.

"No, I want to hear you say that everything will be perfect." He cupped his hand to his ear and waited.

"I have to—"

"Ah-ah-ah." Lance Dumont waved his hand, cutting her off. "Repeat after me . . . it sounds perfect."

He shushed her when she tried to speak again, and Hannah, although she didn't for one second believe it, finally forced the words out—because he would not hear otherwise. "It sounds perfect."

He smiled and nodded, pleased with her performance.

It sounded terrible.

"All I really wanted to do is make sure you're comfortable and your accommodations are to your liking."

"Everything is great." She exaggerated her smile. "Just wonderful, but—"

"All right, I'll catch up with you two in a couple of days." He backed away from the door. "Take your time and enjoy yourselves and I'll be in touch. Here—" he pulled out a business card and handed it to her. "Give me a call if there's anything you need. Alo-HA!"

"Okay, thanks." Hannah took the card, and before she had a chance to add another word, he was gone. "See you later. I guess."

Hannah leaned against the door, closing it. This was trouble, real trouble. What was she going to do? She'd lied, plain and simple. Lied and Hannah couldn't keep lying. She couldn't pretend she had a husband.

She glanced at the card he'd given her. His work phone number, the same number she already had, which meant an explanation would have to wait until tomorrow.

Hannah collapsed into the sofa. Why hadn't she told him? She had her chance . . . sort of. The traveling, the time change, and the lying were all exhausting. They were taking their toll.

She looked down at her hand. What she was really looking at were the rings on the third finger of her left hand. There was the small diamond engagement ring she'd worn for years, but just before coming on this trip she'd slipped on the matching wedding band, thinking she'd need it.

That was a joke.

Christine was right, Earl never loved her.

Hannah slipped off the rings and dropped them onto the coffee table next to a flyer. The flyer said:

Meet Doctor Jerry!

Doctor Jerry sounded like some radio talk show psychologist. That's what she needed, a session with Doctor Jerry might help her or help straighten everything out. What advice would he give?

Dump the creep. Give ole Earl the heave-ho, like he did to you.

Doctor Jerry was right, Earl could take a flying leap. He was the one who got her into this mess in the first place. He was the one who wanted to get married and he was the one who put her on hold.

She was stupid for ever loving him, for trusting him, for believing him. Why would he marry her just because she'd won a contest? He's had his chance . . . five year's worth of chances.

He could take a flying leap.

Glancing at the second line of the flyer it said:

See the stars of Maui.

Doctor Jerry wasn't a shrink but an astronomer. It didn't matter, Hannah liked his advice anyway.

She marched over to the luggage and gave Earl's green pom-pommed bag a swift kick.

Kicking it was too good for him—his luggage. This was it, he'd put her in tough spots before but he'd never left her in anything as bad as this, and she'd never let him do it to her again. She pocketed the flyer, hefted the thirty-six-inch, soft-sided bag and headed out the door and out of the building.

Down on the beach, Hannah grasped the handle with both hands and swung the bag around and around, building up speed. She finally let go and watched it fly into the ocean, where it made a nice, crisp, satisfying splash.

"Alo-HA, Earl."

Jeremy strolled up the northern path of the Wailea Neilani Resort. The coconut palm fronds alongside the path swayed in the gentle island breeze.

The soothing sound of the surf washing up on the beach came from the west. To the east he could make out the muted lights of the hotel rooms. Above him was his future, deep, dark, and endless with possibilities.

Too bad he wasn't able to do anything about it. He was stuck on a deserted beach while his colleagues worked toward the success he wanted so much. He needed to prove that he wasn't the deadbeat failure his father had labeled him.

He wouldn't be proving anything here at this resort that was for sure. And he didn't need to log in anymore time as a beach bum. Jeremy would have liked this maybe five years ago, but not now. Now he was ready to work, but that, as they say, hadn't been written in the stars.

If he had to take his shift playing amateur astronomer he wouldn't whine about it. He'd do the task and get back to the observatory, Keck. After all, it was only a week.

Taking a second glance around, Jeremy saw her walking on the path silhouetted against the light. He recognized the woman who had collided into him in the lobby that afternoon. She was walking right toward him, and she was alone. Okay, so he wasn't the only person on this stretch of beach, but he certainly wouldn't mind her kind of company.

"Hello, again."

"Hello," she said, as an automatic response. "Oh, hello." Recognition flickered in her eyes. The warmer, more genuine reply came when she'd gotten a good look at him. "Aren't you the one who—"

"Stopped you from taking the plunge?" He smiled and she laughed.

"I think I was in shock. I'm sorry. I didn't thank you. I didn't even have a chance to get your name."

"It's Jeremy, Jeremy Gordon." He held out his hand to her.

"Hannah Roberts." She pulled a strand of her loose wavy brown hair off her face.

All of a sudden everything around him felt like it had just clicked. Into the right place. Perfect. Cosmically correct.

Him and her, standing on the beach, on the edge of an island in the middle of the Pacific Ocean. The moment seemed to have frozen in time.

Off to his right the sun sunk below the horizon, shooting off rays of orange and red into the clouds, putting on a light show just for them.

Hannah was much cuter than Jeremy had remembered. "I guess you're here for—"

"Vacation," she answered quickly, cutting him off.

She said *vacation* not *honeymoon,* which meant she was available.

"What are you doing out here all by yourself?" she asked him.

"I'm checking out the area. I'm the resort's resident astronomer for the week."

"Astronomer?" Hannah pulled the flyer from her pocket and handed it to him.

See the stars of Maui.

"Are you Doctor Jerry?"

"*Doctor Jerry?*" Jeremy skimmed the flyer. "Yeah, I guess that would be me."

His first impulse would be to kill those guys at

the observatory and the second was how nice the name sounded when Hannah said it. *Jerry.*

"I think the guys at work thought *Doctor Jerry* sounded less stuffy, friendlier."

"I think you're very friendly." She glanced at him and an exquisite smile graced her face. "Even if your name is really Jeremy."

"I don't think it'll matter what my name is, you're not going to convince anyone to come out here in the middle of the night while they're on vacation to look at the sky. Some of these people are on their honeymoons. I'm sure they have better things to do."

"I think you'll have more than a few people showing up. I know I would."

"You would?"

"Sure. Will you really be able to see anything?"

"I'll have some telescopes set up, of course, and this really is an ideal spot for viewing." A large clear, flat area with the coconut trees blocking the ambient hotel light. "There aren't any city lights to wash out the stars with the ocean over there."

"What can you see from here?"

"I guess first on the viewing list will be Jupiter and a couple of constellations. It's always a good place to start, everyone knows the Big Dipper."

"You can really see a planet?" Hannah stared

up. She wouldn't see them now, but she looked beautiful, looking at the sky.

"Oh, sure. Jupiter will be over the horizon by nine P.M. With the telescopes you'll be able to see Jupiter's banding, maybe its red spot, and several moons."

"You're kidding." She gazed from him back to the sky. No matter how hard she looked she'd never be able to see them.

Why did she sound so amazed? Hadn't she ever looked through a telescope before?

"Doctor Gordon?" a voice called out. "Are you out here? Doctor Gordon?"

"Over here," he answered, facing the approaching person.

One of the hotel employees jogged out to him and handed him a piece of paper. "It's the observatory."

"Okay, thanks." Jeremy glanced at Hannah and regretted that he had to leave. "I guess I'd better go."

"I guess," she whispered.

"Maybe I'll see you around." Jeremy was pulled away from the only thing he was really excited about—Hannah Roberts.

"Maybe," she repeated. "I'll be stopping by to see Saturn and Jupiter for sure."

"I guess I'll see you tomorrow night." He turned from her and headed for the hotel. Jeremy could hardly wait until tomorrow. There was nothing he liked better than seeing a heavenly body.

Hannah woke early that morning after spending half the night weeding Earl's stuff out and salvaging her stuff out of her suitcase. She remembered, too late, that she'd left Earl alone with the suitcases while he said he'd been doing a little *repacking*—just before they'd left for the airport.

What had he done with her pink short-sleeved, flowered cotton dress and her new white strappy sandals she'd bought especially for the trip? He'd put some of his clothes in her suitcase and hers in his. Which meant some of her clothes must have been in the suitcase she'd tossed into the Pacific Ocean last night.

Swapping her favorite flowered pink cotton dress with Earl's *Official Bikini Inspector* T-shirt was not a fair trade. She couldn't believe that he thought that was perfect beach attire.

Hannah had a few hours until the Heavenly Hawaiian Honeymoon offices opened and figured that would give her enough time to toss the rest of Earl's garbage and take a walk on the beach. She changed into her swimsuit and stepped into a pale yellow terry cover-up.

She placed Earl's things in a shopping bag and headed for the elevator. The doors slid open and on one side a couple cozied up together as she walked in, taking the space of one. Here she was, a single person hogging the spot of one person. Not only was she all by herself, but she really felt alone.

Reaching the ground floor, Hannah waited for the couple to exit before she stepped outside. In the early morning light she could see the surrounding greenery extending from the front lobby engulfed the entire outside of the hotel, changing into manicured gardens with a path that ambled from the hotel to the beachfront.

Couples strolled up and down the garden paths hand in hand even this early in the morning. They sat close together at the open-air restaurant, gazing out at the ocean, and others splashed around the pool. What was Hannah doing in the land of happy couples?

She could have been one of those twosomes, if things would have worked out the way they were supposed to. Hannah and Earl could have been married, one of the newlyweds.

She looked down at her last reminders of Earl in her arms, wishing she could burn them instead of dropping them in a trash can. Setting them on fire would have made her feel much better but the tiki torches were out for the night.

Do it.

Hannah glanced around nonchalantly before dropping the bag into a hotel garbage can, never gave it a second thought, and continued to the beach for her walk.

She traveled past the plumeria- and hibiscus-planted hotel area to the large white sun tents set up by the swimming pools to the warm, sandy beach. She dropped her cover-up on one of the lounge chairs near the pool and headed for the ocean.

"You're not thinking of going in by yourself are you?"

Hannah swung around and saw him. "Oh, hi, Jeremy. Good morning. Isn't the ocean beautiful? I've never seen anything like it." She gazed up and down the shore. "Look at the different blues, greens, aqua, and turquoise in the water."

"It *is* beautiful. I don't usually take a good look at it. Not as closely as you are."

"I could never take this for granted. Feel the breeze, it's just enough to keep it from feeling too warm." She closed her eyes and inhaled the moist salty air. "This is normal?"

"For this time of year."

"I've never seen the ocean before, you know."

"Never?" Jeremy sounded shocked.

"I was born and raised in Kansas. This is the first time I've been out of the state." He didn't know anyone who never left the state where they were born. "Dexter is about as far away from the ocean as you can get but I think it was worth the wait."

Hannah stepped forward and the water washed up on her feet and ankles.

"If you're going into the water you should have a swim buddy." There was a tone of caution in his voice.

"A swim buddy?" *Did he mean she needed to bring a rubber ducky in the water?*

"You know, a swim buddy is someone you go out into the water with so you don't get into trouble."

She stared back at him, wide-eyed. His explanation had been casual but it scared the heck out of her.

"Just in case."

That didn't make Hannah feel any better.

"I won't be going in that far." She moved farther into the water and it hit her mid-calf. "It's so nice and warm, like bath water."

"Suit yourself." He shrugged.

The surf splashed on her thighs and his gaze didn't recede with the water. She could feel him watching her. He was studying her body, as if committing it to memory.

It was a long time since someone other than Earl looked at her like that. *Did Jeremy think she had nice legs?*

"Watch out for the sharks," he said as though he were wishing her a nice day.

"Sharks?" Hannah leaped back, alarmed. In another second she was out of the water and had scampered back next to him. "There aren't really any sharks, are there?"

"Sure there are. It's Hawaii, sharks are big fans of the warm water."

Hannah stared at him. He couldn't have meant it, not really. "You're scaring me."

He draped her hand through his arm and motioned her forward, down the shoreline. "There's nothing to be afraid of. You just have to be careful."

Jeremy walked along the shore with the ocean to one side and Hannah on the other. At first she was uneasy when the water touched her, washed over her feet, ankles, and calves. She was sure there were sharks ready to leap at her from the surf.

"What you really need to do is snorkel."

"Snorkel? You mean with a mask and a—" She motioned from her mouth to above her head, all the while keeping an eye on the ocean.

"Yeah, that's right—a snorkel. That way you can see all the colorful fish."

There were dozens of people out in the water, snorkeling already. Bodies clad in all sorts of bright swimwear dotted the water offshore, moved up and down with the swells, their snorkels poked into the air like mini periscopes.

"There's too many people for there to be fish out there," she said. So if there weren't any fish, what were those people looking at?

"You'd be surprised." He seemed to know that she was curious and wanted to try it. "It's not hard, and I'll be with you the entire time."

"It looks like fun, but I don't swim very well."

"You don't have to know how to swim. All you do is float on the surface of the water and look down. You'll love it."

"The water moves." The water surged with the surf. She was tempted, but still a bit spooked.

"It's pretty easy. You can practice in the pool until you get the hang of it."

"The pool sounds okay, safe." She looked from the snorkelers to Jeremy, deep into his comforting eyes, and knew she would be safe.

Hannah should have felt some sort of guilt. After all, if things had worked out the way they were supposed to she would have been married to Earl instead of making plans with this handsome stranger she'd met yesterday.

She shouldn't, Hannah warned herself. *She really shouldn't.* "Will you be my swim buddy?"

"I won't leave your side." He grinned at her.

She smiled back and nodded without hesitation. "Okay. Let's do it."

"Good for you." Jeremy led the way from the shore and headed back to the hotel. "We'll check out the equipment and you'll be seeing saltwater fish before lunch."

*　*　*

After spending two hours snorkeling in the ocean, Hannah stepped into the calm water of the swimming pool. Jeremy led the way. She'd follow him almost anywhere after being with him where the Hawaiian wildlife swam.

"Just hold your breath," he said. "And we're going to swim through this waterfall."

Of course she trusted him when it came to water safety, he'd been Hannah's swim buddy, starting from the lessons in the pool to the real thing out at sea.

Hannah held her breath and closed her eyes. Jeremy moved through the curtain of water and she felt the heavy drops of the waterfall break over her head. Then—nothing. She opened her eyes, amazed to find herself inside a cave.

Jeremy may have looked better wet than dry. The water slicked back his dark brown curly hair, making his thick eyelashes, that any girl would kill for, black and intense.

Looking back through the waterfall, Hannah could see the outside world. Inside the cave was a submerged bar. They took one of the booths that looked like it was chiseled out of rock. It felt weird to sit at a table while still in water that was up to her waist.

"What can I get you two to drink?" the waitress asked.

Hannah had no idea what to say and looked

over at him. *What kind of place was this? Neptune's watering hole?*

"How about some POG?" he suggested.

"POG?" Or had he said hog?

He cracked a smile when she made a face. "POG is a blend of passion fruit, orange, and guava juices."

"Oh, that sounds good."

Jeremy held up two fingers and said, "Make that two" to the waitress. "And bring—" he gestured, making a circle with his fingers and said something else that Hannah couldn't make out. The waitress seemed to understand and she nodded.

"Can we go back to the ocean again?" Hannah was having a great time. Snorkeling had been the best thing that had happened to her since meeting him. She had decided hours ago that Doctor Jerry was a hottie, he was fit, built, and tanned like an island boy.

"I'm not sure. We've already been out for a couple hours and I don't think you realize how tired you are."

"I don't know about tired, but I'm starved. I think saltwater must make you hungrier than pool water does."

"You're working a lot harder out there than you think. I knew you'd love to snorkel."

"I can't believe how many fish there were. There were a zillion yellow ones."

"Tangs." His eyes narrowed when he smiled.

"And those black and yellow ones with the long—" she made the motion of an antenna-like device from her head.

"Moorish Idols."

"And then the fish with the cute little beaks." Hannah could feel that she was starting to fall for him.

"Parrot fish."

"I think they were my favorite, really colorful." He knew exactly what to do and what to say, so knowledgeable, and so worldly. Was falling for your shrink a Freudian thing?

Jeremy wasn't a psychologist, he was an astronomer. She wished she had remembered more about him from the first time they met.

The waitress returned with their drinks, which sported little colored paper umbrellas, and a plate of appetizers.

"Is this for us?"

"You said you were hungry."

"Can I eat this pineapple?" She stared at him wide-eyed, not sure what to devour first.

"It's meant to be garnish, but, yeah, it's edible. Go ahead."

Hannah popped a piece of pineapple into her mouth followed by one of the appetizers. "Yum . . . What is this?" She pointed to her mouth and hoped he'd answer fast so she could eat another.

"Pupus."

She stopped chewing and stared at him as if she'd taken a bite of. . . .

"No, it's all right," he reassured her. "Pupus are appetizers."

"Oh, I thought you meant—"

"No, they're just appetizers." He ate another and washed it down. "Little egg rolls"—those she recognized—"Shumai, gyoza"—he pointed at each on the plate—"Cubed honey roasted pork, and various other tidbits."

"It's not fish, is it?"

Jeremy looked down at the platter. "Some of it might be, I don't know."

"I'm never going to eat fish again." She announced with conviction.

"Come on . . ."

"How can I? After seeing those graceful, beautiful fish this morning I couldn't."

"Oh, I see. Well, the fish they serve in restaurants are from deep in the ocean, they're clumsy and ugly—the perfect eating fish."

Hannah sipped her POG—it was wonderful. The blended fruit juice was the perfect tropical drink—sweet, fresh, and flavorful.

Nearly an hour later Hannah set her empty glass on the table and Jeremy helped her clear the pupu platter.

"You're right, now that I'm full, I'm tired." She

closed her eyes and leaned her head back. With all the exercise, food, and drink, Hannah was feeling no pain. "I can't tell you what a good time I've had today."

"It was fun, wasn't it?"

He placed his hand over hers, reminding Hannah how strong he was. Just as he promised, not once had he let go of her hand while they were in the water. She'd felt safe and comfortable and, right now, she could have fallen asleep where she sat.

"And today's not over yet," he continued.

Hannah straightened and stared at him through her relaxed eyelids. "It isn't?"

"I've still got to go to work tonight."

"I nearly forgot." Hannah felt sorry for him. She was exhausted and couldn't imagine trying to do anything except sleep. "Aren't you beat?"

"I'll catnap and be ready for tonight. I'm used to it. I normally work late hours. You're going to be there, right?"

A chance to see him again? "I wouldn't miss it." Hannah felt his hand tighten infinitesimally, she still had hold of his arm, and then he was staring into her eyes. She knew he wanted to kiss her, and she wanted to kiss him, too . . . but she shouldn't, she'd only just met him.

Hannah blinked and pulled back, breaking the moment. "I'd better let you get your catnap, and I think I could use one, too."

How simple it would have been to invite him to her room, and how she wanted to . . . but she didn't know him.

She could have so easily curled up against his warm, strong body and slept, but it was too soon.

The wound Earl had created left her uncertain of the choices she'd made. What Hannah did know is that she should not be making any kind of decision when it concerned men.

Chapter Three

Hannah's phone rang as she stepped inside her room. "Hello?"

"It's Christine."

It felt good to hear a friendly voice. Hannah slid onto the sofa. "Hey, girl, what are you doing? Why aren't you with Tim?" From what Hannah had seen, honeymooners at the Neilani were joined at the hip.

"Tim is having a scuba lesson in the pool and I'm checking up on you."

"Come on. I don't need you to do that."

"Someone needs to keep an eye on you. Did Earl call you and apologize?"

"No." Hannah had nearly forgotten about him.

Earl was the last person she wanted to hear from or think about. He was out of her life forever. "He's history."

"Good. I'm glad to hear that. Don't you forgive him. Ever." Christine sounded adamant. "Did you talk to the contest people yet?"

Hannah gasped and covered her mouth instead of pounding her fist against her head or her head against the wall. "Oh, my gosh. I forgot all about it." She glanced around the posh living room, looking for a clock. "What time is it?"

There was a pause before Christine said, "four-fifty-seven."

"Almost five o'clock? Oh, great . . . they're almost closed." How? How could Hannah have forgotten about the contest people?

"What happened? I thought you were going to call them right away?"

"I was. I did . . . I called them when I got in yesterday, but they were closed and I was going to call first thing this morning." Hannah had every intention of doing it, she would have done it but . . . it didn't happen. She got distracted.

"It was so early when I got up this morning, hours before they opened, so I thought I had time for a walk on the beach."

"You shouldn't go into the water by yourself, it's dangerous out there," Christine lectured her like a big sister. "There are things in there . . . eels, jellyfish, stingrays, and even sharks."

"That's what Jeremy said, so we were swim buddies, and he showed me how to snorkel in the pool this morning and then we did the water-slides for a while. Then we snorkeled in the ocean for a couple of hours and after we went to the swim-up bar. I guess it really hit me how tired I was, so I came back to my room and I thought I might—"

"Wait-wait-wait a sec." There was a long pause. "A swim-up bar? And who's this guy?"

"I met Jeremy here at the hotel. He stopped me from falling into a pond in the lobby yesterday." That really sounded bad, even for Hannah.

"You fell into a pond?"

"No, Jeremy caught me. It really would have been embarrassing if he hadn't."

"I should think." Christine didn't say anything more but Hannah could hear the concern in her friend's voice. And maybe she had a right to be a little worried.

"He's an astronomer from the Big Island, that's what he calls the main island, Hawaii. He works at one of the observatories there and this week he's showing all the guests at the resort some planets and other stuff out in space."

"So you like this Jeremy guy, huh?"

There was no hiding anything from Christine, and if Hannah could listen to herself she'd admit that she was gushing over him. But she couldn't help it, she'd never met anyone as interesting as Jeremy. He just seemed to know a lot about things, and life.

"He's . . ." Hannah didn't know what to say. "Nice." That was an okay thing to say. She liked him. "I need to call the contest people, maybe someone is still there."

"Okay, but you have to promise to call me right back and let me know what's going on between you two." Hannah could tell that Christine didn't want to let her go. She wanted to know everything Hannah knew about Jeremy right now.

Hannah agreed and hung up. She immediately dialed the Heavenly Hawaiian Honeymoon office and prayed someone was working late. No such luck, no one answered, and there was no answering machine.

Hannah hung up and the light on her phone blinked, telling her that she had a message. She followed the directions, punching a couple of buttons to retrieve her missed call.

"Alo-HA, Mr. and Mrs. Henderson, this is Lance Dumont from Heavenly Hawaiian Honeymoons."

Oh, great. While Hannah was calling him, he was calling her, and got a busy signal.

"I'll be stopping in first thing tomorrow morning to see you for the interview. I hope you're working on a nice tan for the pictures. We'll be there around ten. See you tomorrow."

Ten o'clock? Pictures? Lance Dumont was coming in the morning. Hannah's head swam. *What was she going to do?* She was scared, felt trapped.

If he'd made that leap on his own when they first met she was sure he could do it a second time. But this time she might give him a little help.

All she had to do was make it *look* like Earl was still there. Hannah looked around. It was much too neat a room for Earl to have lived in.

When Earl was around there was a constant mess with socks, shoes, and shirts strewn about. It wasn't a difficult adjustment to make, but there was something Hannah was missing—Earl's clothes.

Now she needed them. Too bad she hadn't known before she chucked them in the ocean last night or when she dumped them in the garbage this morning. But the way she was feeling who could blame her?

She didn't have a choice; she had to get some new ones. There were hotel clothing stores downstairs where she could shop. Hannah grabbed her purse and headed out.

Dragging herself into the Island Outfitter, she tried to decide what Earl needed. A swift kick in the tush is what she came up with, or a two by four across the top of his head would do.

Shopping for Earl proved harder than she thought. He didn't deserve new clothes, and she had trouble mentally dressing the deadbeat.

A deep purple Aloha shirt caught her eye. The flowers were colorful without being too feminine and the pineapples were cheery and fun.

Wouldn't Jeremy look good in that?

Dressing Jeremy was far easier and more fun than torturing herself over Earl. And really, Lance Dumont wouldn't know the difference between Earl-type and Jeremy-type clothes.

She checked the labels and pulled out a size large that should have been the right size for his broad shoulders. *Look at those cute tropical shorts.* A khaki cotton drawstring pair went into her basket. *How about undies? Boxers or briefs?*

Hannah closed her eyes for a little private daydream. She sighed.

Definitely a briefs man. And she mentally sang to herself: *I see London, I see France. . . .*

And even though he might wear colorful Aloha shirts on the outside, something told her that underneath he'd be strictly the white cotton type.

She snagged a package of men's underwear, size 34s. On the way to the counter she snagged a pair of rubber flip-flops, heck, she grabbed a second pair, she needed them too. It's an island must. And when she turned around she saw him.

"Doing some shopping?" Jeremy said with a big smile.

Hannah wadded the men's clothing she carried, hoping he hadn't noticed her purchases.

"Yeah, I thought I would pick up a couple things. You know some touristy stuff."

"Nice choice of color," he said, lifting a shirt sleeve. "Did you get the plastic fish guide? You can take it in the water with you and it has pictures of reef fish with their names."

"Sounds like a great idea, I'll have to check it out. You're going up to take a catnap?"

"I'm headed for my room now. I needed some toothpaste—ran out. You want to go first?" He motioned for her to go ahead of him in the cashier's line.

"No, thanks. I'm still looking around." She moved away to the far wall, picking up an extra toothbrush, comb, razor, and shaving cream to round out her purchases.

He pulled out his wallet to pay. "See you later tonight, right?"

"You can count on it." *Just after I finish staging my little deception.*

Jeremy waved good-bye to her on his way out. The knot in Hannah's stomach was sending a message. She had to stop lying. She wasn't good at it, didn't feel good about it, and if she didn't quit, she would certainly get caught.

Sunset was at 6:16 P.M. and the sky-watching program started at nine. Jeremy led Luka to the secluded spot on the north side of the resort.

"It's nice of you to help me, Luka. Are you going to be back at eleven to help me pack up?"

"Yeah, sure. You need help. I help you." Luka made it sound so simple.

"We'll set up over there." Jeremy pointed to a clearing, putting them on the edge of the grass and the beach sand.

Luka opened the first box and Jeremy pulled out the contents.

"First you need to set up the tripod." Jeremy extended the legs and set it on the ground.

"—pod, yeah."

"Then you pull out the scope and set it on top of the tripod."

"—scope, yeah."

"Take off these first." Jeremy spun the wing nuts off and lowered the telescope onto the tripod. "Then anchor the scope by screwing them back on. That's it, right there—make sure it's tight. I'll take care of the eyepieces and tracking equipment."

"The quip-ment?"

"Nevermind. You can help me out by setting up

the scopes. Two there, two there, and two there."
Jeremy pointed out the three stations.

"Yeah, can do."

Luka opened the second box and Jeremy went
to work on attaching the tracking cables and eyepieces. His hands might have been busy with the
equipment but his mind was on Hannah.

Hannah was something special, and he couldn't
wait to see her again. He'd have to work at not ignoring the other guests. That is, if there were any
other guests that bothered to show up. It'd be fine
with him if she were the only one there.

There'd be nothing he'd like better than to
spend an evening with her curled up in one of
those giant webbed hammocks hung between the
tall, looming palms.

They could lay among the swaying trees and
half dozen telescopes, enjoying the evening as it
turned to night, watching the palm fronds sway in
the gentle breeze, and talk about tropical fish.

It would be the perfect way to spend an evening.

Jeremy smiled. He wanted to see Hannah again,
couldn't wait to see her again. He looked up at
Luka. "You know who I saw today?" He just
couldn't keep it to himself.

"A two-headed Moray eel?" Luka guessed.

"No."

"An albino Nene?"

"No."

"A Humuhumunukunukuapua'a?"

"No."

"Who, *den?*" Luka gave up and stared at Jeremy.

"Hannah Roberts."

"Who?"

"That woman I nearly knocked into the pond in the lobby yesterday."

"Oh, Koi bait." Luka opened another box and pulled out a tripod.

"Koi—" Jeremy had to chuckle at Luka. Local Hawaiians and their Pidgin English, their slang, it was too funny the words they came up with. "Yeah, her. We went snorkeling this morning, and then we had lunch. She's really something, you know. I had a great time with her."

"*Aznuts.*"

"What's crazy about it? I'm an all right guy. She could do a lot worse than me."

"You *lolo.* She's a honeymooner. *Wid anudder* guy, you know."

"Honeymoon?" Boy, did Luka have things mixed up. "She's not on her honeymoon, she's here on vacation. Alone."

"She won that big honeymoon prize from the Island boys."

No, it couldn't be true. Hannah couldn't be on her honeymoon because she . . . because she would have been with her husband not spending the day with him.

Wasn't she coming on to him this morning? Maybe not coming on to him, exactly, but she was at least showing some interest. He thought back to the way she looked at him.

Luka had to be all mixed up, confused. But then again maybe not.

Come to think of it, when Jeremy bumped into her later that afternoon in the clothing store she didn't seem that thrilled to see him, she seemed nervous. She didn't want to talk to him, and now that he thought about it, she was a little more than anxious to get away from him.

At the time he thought she had been wrapped up with shopping, but now he wasn't sure what had gone on. The uneasiness started in his stomach and worked its way up to his throat. There was more to her nervousness than he thought.

What had she been carrying? Clothes? A shirt? Pants? No, shorts. Were they men's? Flip-flops? Uni-sex . . . but there had been two pair not one. One for her and one for. . . .

No, it couldn't be true.

There was no way she would leave her husband on her honeymoon, and she certainly would not be seeing other guys. She wasn't that devious. She'd make a loving and devoted wife, Jeremy was sure.

How did he know? He thought she was single and up for grabs. Hannah Roberts had Jeremy fooled.

"Hey, *brah? Brah*-man, wake up." Luka nudged Jeremy on the shoulder.

"What?" Jeremy glanced at Luka and a half-dozen tripods, standing like a grove of small trees.

"All *pau.*"

"What?"

"All *pau.*"

"All finished? Okay." Jeremy looked at the tripods around him, set up in the exact places where he had asked. "Great, thanks."

"*Bodda* you?"

"No, it doesn't bother me at all. I haven't even given it a second thought." Five or six maybe. But thinking about Hannah had to stop now. If she was married then Jeremy was out of the picture.

Ouch. What a way to find out.

Hannah and Jeremy . . . all *pau.*

"About time you called me back," Christine scolded Hannah nearly three hours after they last spoke. "Tim just brought in a flyer about *Stargazing with Doctor Jerry* at your hotel. Is your Jeremy this Doctor Jerry?"

"Yeah, that's him." Just talking about him made Hannah feel all tingly.

"Tim says he wants to go, so I guess we can meet you and all walk over there together, okay?"

"I guess that's fine," Hannah agreed. She was going and didn't mind if Christine and Tim joined her. And she really would like to know what her best friend had to say about her new guy.

"And before I forget—pencil me in for lunch tomorrow. I'll meet you in the Grand Dining Room at twelve-thirty. Is that a good time for you?"

"Tim's not going to join us?"

"He's still busy with those scuba lessons. Yesterday, they practiced in the pool, today they're going out in the ocean. They sailed out early this morning. Besides, there's no way I'm going into the ocean on one of those rubber raft things. I'd much rather have lunch with you."

Although Hannah would have given it a go, *Adventurous* was not Christine's middle name.

"Anyway . . . I hear the Neilani has the best brunch on the island."

"I'm not sure, Christine. Jeremy might have other plans for us." Hannah could imagine they might spend the morning snorkeling, but by lunch they might be free. "Let me check with him first."

"You said, 'plans for *us.*' That sounds so sweet. You bring him along. I want to really check this guy out."

"Christine—you're married." That's all Hannah needed was her friend to hog all the good men. One per woman was all that should be allowed. There weren't enough of them to go around as it was.

"Not for me, for you. I want to make sure his intentions are honorable."

"Honorable? They don't have to be honorable. We're just spending some time together. You know, keeping each other company. We're not involved, not even thinking of getting serious. You can forget about us getting married."

"Who says?" Christine's tone sounded like teasing but Hannah knew better.

"I only met him yesterday and . . . really, Christine . . . I don't even know him." As much as Hannah liked Jeremy marriage wasn't even on the horizon.

"What does 'how-long-you've-known-him' have to do with it? You knew what's-his-face for years and he turned out to be a bum."

"Earl did not turn into a bum." Hannah defended him—it wasn't something she felt strongly about, but she thought someone should do it.

"You're right, he was *always* a bum." Christine amended. "You just never saw it."

"And you did?" *If Christine was such a good friend and she new Earl was bad for her, why hadn't she said anything*? Hannah already knew the answer to that—she wanted them to remain friends.

"You were too much in love with him to hear any different. I never thought he was good enough for you. Let's just hope Doctor Jerry turns out better."

Better?

Better wouldn't be a word Hannah would choose

to describe him. As they said in Hawaii, Jeremy *no ka oi*—simply put, it meant he was the best.

It was difficult for Hannah to tell the difference between regular stars and the planets. She was right about other people's interest in looking through Jeremy's telescopes that first night stargazing. It must have been a real shock to him that six couples showed up.

"No, not that one, the really bright one to the right and up." Jeremy pointed up and outward, capturing everyone's attention.

The lone tiki torch gave off enough light so no one bumped into each other. Hannah wouldn't mind bumping into Jeremy. If she had been really lucky no one would have shown up tonight, and they would be here alone.

"That's Jupiter. If you want to see its moons, we're going to have to look quick. It's going down soon."

"Below the horizon," one of the men said to the woman with him.

"You can see a bit of the red spot and four of the moons through these two telescopes."

The couples gathered around the two telescopes, waiting their turn to take a peek.

"See the stars that make a big V?" Jeremy said to the guests waiting in line to see Jupiter. "That's the head of the bull in the constellation of Taurus. If you look off to the right . . . See that group of stars?"

They all nodded.

"That's a star cluster known as the Pleiades or the Seven Sisters. They're the shoulders of the bull. You can take a closer look at them through those two telescopes over there."

The first woman who peered into the telescope reached out for her husband. "Ooh, there *are* a bunch of stars there, look honey." She pulled him near for his turn at the telescope.

Hannah studied Jeremy's profile illuminated by the soft light of the tiki torch. It was just enough to carve the basic shape of his face, leaving her to fill in the outline of his eyes and mouth.

Two couples moved from the Jupiter line to the next set of telescopes.

"Is that the bull?" one of the men asked.

Hannah could have sworn Jeremy looked right at her on his way to pointing out the constellation for the man and his wife.

"The head is that way"—the man pointed to the left—"and the tail at the other?"

"Hi, Jeremy," she mouthed and all he did was look at her. No wave, no nod, nothing.

Of course he was busy, and a few more couples had joined them, making the total couple count eight and person count sixteen, not counting Jeremy or Hannah.

But it felt more than just "being busy" it felt like he was ignoring her. Like he didn't want to see her.

Jeremy moved to the last two telescopes. "These are pointed at the Crab Nebula." A line began to form behind the last station even before he had finished the explanation. "It's located between the top two stars of the bull's horns."

One woman looked at the nebula and commented, "It's all fuzzy."

"A nebula is a cloud of gas and dust from an exploding star. History reports that in 1054 this explosion was so powerful that it was seen during the day."

The woman took a second look then chatted with the people behind her. Hannah took advantage of the break in questions to speak to him.

"You have quite a turnout." Her smile was probably invisible in the darkness. "I bet there's more people here than you thought would turn up."

"Yes, there are," he replied, much cooler than Hannah would have expected.

"Doctor Jerry?" one of the women who'd just arrived called.

"Excuse me," Jeremy said and walked away from Hannah.

There was no excuse for his behavior. Hannah didn't know what was wrong. They'd spent a wonderful day together, so wonderful that she was thinking they'd end the evening with a kiss.

The only kiss she'd get was a kiss-off. Another one.

One yesterday and one today.

Hannah shouldn't have felt as bad as she did, she hadn't known Jeremy all that well. She wasn't in love with him or anything. And she knew him what—for a whole day?

Only a day.

And he didn't really save her life. She'd never have drowned in that lobby pond. It was only a shallow pool of water. She could have stood up and walked out—wet and a little humiliated—but alive.

It didn't matter, not really. He wasn't important to her, and it was clear that she meant nothing to him.

But no matter what she told herself, it did hurt. She wondered what had caused him to act this way.

A woman waved at him while her husband took his turn looking through the telescope. "Did you have a question?" Jeremy stopped next to the couple.

"I have a question about Taurus."

"I'll do my best to answer."

"I was wondering if you can tell me if Taurus and Gemini are compatible?"

Jeremy looked from the woman, stared straight at Hannah, and replied, "Not if one of them is married."

Chapter Four

Even in the sporadic flicker of the torch's light Jeremy could see Hannah's eyes widen. She covered her mouth, shocked that her secret was out.

He was an idiot. How could he have not known she was married? How could he have known? She never gave any indication.

Not once had he caught Hannah looking over her shoulder, waiting to be caught by her husband. Jeremy thought she was sugar and spice and completely unattached—they were having a good time.

Hannah sure was having a good time playing him for a chump, and Jeremy should have kept his head in the nebula and remembered that Earth girls were easy.

He hadn't seen Hannah leave, but the next time

he looked back she was gone. Without an explanation or apology she'd left and that confirmed her guilt.

What he really needed to do was get back to work. He should never have let her distract him. And as insignificant as this job was, this was work for the moment.

Jeremy shook off any thoughts of his personal problems and headed back to the first set of scopes to answer questions.

Preparing for the next constellation, Jeremy lined the first scope up with Orion. Looking through the eyepiece he searched for any of the three stars of the belt. The markers he searched for were Zeta Orionis, the left-most star, then down to Sigma Orionis, below the belt, and below that the Crab Nebula.

But inside, sadness settled around his heart. He missed Hannah. He wanted her here with him. He wanted to know what she would have thought of Jupiter's moon and the Pleiades in Taurus.

He had a sneaking suspicion that seeing them would have been something new for her. And although he hated to admit it and found it hard to explain, Jeremy felt the same rush of adrenaline when seeing something new through Hannah's eyes.

Catching Delta Orionis, the right-most star in his sights, Jeremy swung downward toward his target nebula, and stopped. *What was that, to the right of Eta Orionis?*

The space there looked . . . wrong.

How could space look *wrong?*

Something about that region looked different. A barely discernable area lit a bit brighter than it should be, and his gut feeling told him it didn't look quite right.

Probably nothing.

Jeremy moved on, locking the tracking system onto the Crab Nebula. A few minutes later he gave the Constellation Orion talk, emphasizing its binary stars.

The next few hours crawled by and thoughts of Hannah kept coming back. He'd fallen for her—a married woman, a *newly* married woman. Nothing he could do about it. She was off-limits and he needed to forget about her.

Luka returned as promised to help Jeremy pack up for the night. They didn't talk much and no one brought up Hannah's name.

Jeremy hesitated before dismantling the last scope. He wanted to take a quick peek at Eta Orionis . . . or rather what was near Eta Orionis.

He peered into the eyepiece and made his way across Orion's belt down to Eta Orionis. Nothing was there, but the area next to it still didn't look right. Jeremy removed the eyepiece and unscrewed the flex cable from the unit.

Maybe out of curiosity he'd give Russell a call at the observatory and have him check on it.

Hannah woke the next morning, sad, exhausted, and emotionally drained. She hadn't slept all night. She couldn't forget the hurt, betrayed look in Jeremy's eyes. And on top of that, she was the one who'd caused it.

He *knew* she was married. But she really wasn't.

Now she sat among Earl's scattered, pretend clothes, feeling miserable, waiting for Lance Dumont.

What did she think she was doing? She hadn't wanted to fool him. She wanted to explain what happened. Hannah must have been more than tired yesterday, she must have been delirious. *What had she been thinking?*

Earl wasn't here. Why would she pretend otherwise? She couldn't—wouldn't lie to Lance Dumont, not on purpose.

And, in a perfect world, she would have liked Jeremy to know the truth.

Trying to cover for an absent Earl had been a horrible idea. *Why did she ever think to do this?* It wasn't like her.

Hannah straightened the skirt of her sundress and headed to the sofa to pick up the khaki shorts lying over the arm and collect the flip-flops kicked under the coffee table.

A knock on the door sounded on her way to snatching up the white briefs she'd carefully tossed in the far corner where Earl wouldn't have had a second thought to dumping them.

"Alo-HA," Lance Dumont greeted her as soon as Hannah opened the door. Another man stood behind him with a large, professional-looking camera in hand.

Hannah glanced down at her bare feet, feeling a bit vulnerable. *Was it already ten? Where had the time gone?*

"Am I early?" He looked from the bundle of clothes in her arms to his wristwatch. "You're on your honeymoon, you don't have to clean up on my behalf."

If she hadn't felt bad enough before, him thinking she was a slob didn't make her feel any better.

Hannah swiped at her nose, holding back the tears that threatened to fall. She was going to have her say. "I have to be honest with you—"

"I take it your husband isn't here." He glanced behind her, inside the suite, to the rest of the mess.

"No, he's not. Earl is—"

"Please, I can see you're upset." Lance waved the photographer away. "I think we need to leave you two to patch things up."

Hannah could feel him backing down but she didn't want him to leave yet. She wanted to tell him everything, explain.

"Really," he assured her. "You don't have to say another word. Being married is a big step and sometimes it's not an easy one to take."

"Yes, but—" Hannah tried to continue. Her spent tears of sadness were changing into tears of fear and frustration. He had to let her speak.

"I'll call again." He held up his hand, stopping her. "Don't worry, we have plenty of time." With that Lance Dumont and his photographer left.

Hannah had herself a good cry in the shower. By the time she had dressed, in one of the dresses she'd brought from home, and brushed her hair she had pulled herself together.

She slipped on a pair of sandals before heading to the Grand Dining Room of her hotel to meet Christine. Hannah passed under the pergola filling the main floor of the lobby and walked around the meandering pond.

Off to the right, the twin marble and brass staircases flanked a stage where the live music originated. Band members dressed in neat slacks and matching Aloha shirts crooned a blend of oldies, top 40 tunes, and Hawaiian ballads.

Turning left into the endless dining room, Hannah decided that finding Christine was going to be harder than she thought. The restaurant went on and on, room after room, with station after station of various breakfast and luncheon foods.

"Hannah!" Christine caught her attention from a table not far from the entrance. She waved Hannah over and looked around. "Where's your Jeremy?"

Hannah set her purse on the table and slid into the chair next to Christine. "I don't think he's *my* Jeremy anymore."

"No? What happened?"

"He *thinks* I'm on my honeymoon." Hannah felt a little drab in her Midwestern sundress next to her friend's brightly colored Hawaiian equivalent, decorated with red and orange hibiscus flowers.

"How did he find out?"

"I don't know." But Hannah didn't feel like wearing brightly colored anything. Right now her dress reflected her mood, drab and dreary.

"I think having a guy think you're married would pretty much ruin any potential of a romantic relationship." Christine pointed to the nearby food station. "Let's get in line before it gets any longer."

Christine led the way to the first breakfast island. Hannah passed on the scrambled and poached eggs, bacon, ham, and Portuguese sausage. The fruits, cereals, and beverage bar held more interest for her.

Choosing was hard enough between orange, apple, and tomato juice, but tropical juices, including pineapple, guava, and mango was almost more than she could handle. The crepes, pancakes, and French toast barely fit on Christine's plate, making the return to their table sooner rather than later.

"Okay." Christine draped her crisp, white linen napkin across her lap and picked up her fork and knife, readying herself. "I want you to tell me everything that happened last night."

Jeremy could barely look at the fresh sliced pineapple. It was one of Hannah's favorites. She always ate the pineapple garnish off both their plates and she thought papaya tasted like cheerful cantaloupe. He chuckled at the time but without Hannah near to say the words it wasn't so funny.

That had happened yesterday, before he found out that she was married. But today Jeremy wondered why she had shared her papaya experience with him and not her new husband.

Around a large, multi-protea flower arrangement of the luncheon island, Jeremy saw Hannah sitting, not with her husband, but another woman, a blond. Hannah didn't look very happy.

Jeremy shouldn't have cared. He should ignore her, but he couldn't.

The women had their heads bent close, it was obvious they were busy with secret, confidential girl-talk. Anything to do with Hannah was none of his business. She was married and that was that.

Jeremy moved to a food island only a few tables away from Hannah and peered over the top of a pineapple, in a tropical fruit display near her table.

He wasn't really listening, he was taking his time spooning frittata onto his plate.

"Being married isn't all it's cracked up to be, is it?" Hannah's friend sat back in her chair and smiled. "I want to know what's going to happen when people start finding out that you're not married."

The serving spoon slipped out of Jeremy's hand and clattered onto the metal serving dishes. He caught it in time to keep it from bouncing around, making any more noise, and then he ducked so Hannah wouldn't see him.

Not married? Had he heard right? Hannah wasn't married?

But Luka had said— It didn't matter what Luka said, he must have been wrong.

Now that Jeremy knew the truth, realization of what he'd done, how he had treated her hit him. He'd been terrible to her last night. Could she ever forgive him?

"You could do worse than not being married," Christine told Hannah.

"I don't think Lance Dumont will think so." Holding her papaya still with her fork, Hannah sliced it into four pieces with her knife.

"Who's he?"

"Lance Dumont is the contest guy from the

magazine. He's been trying to set up a meeting with *my husband* and me since I got here. Just this morning he stopped by to see us."

"Oh, Hannah." Christine gave Hannah a sympathetic look that made Hannah want to burst into a second bout of tears.

"Last night I threw some clothes around the place, you know, like Earl used to. You've seen his place." Just talking about it made Hannah's stomach feel all tied up in knots. "I tried to make it look like he was living there with me."

"You meant you lied about you and Earl? About Earl being here?"

"I was going to but—I couldn't go through with it." Hannah had tried her best.

"Good for you. It's not like you to behave that way. You couldn't be dishonest."

"I don't have to be. He caught me as I was picking up and made up his own reasons why Earl wasn't there." Hannah felt the disappointment and frustration all over again. "I tried to tell him, really I did."

"Do you mean you still haven't told him the truth?" Christine could not have been more shocked. Hannah was there, living it, for gosh sakes, she'd tried her best.

"He never gave me a chance."

"Oh, Hannah." Christine set her fork on the table and shook her head like she didn't believe what she was hearing. "It's hard to believe it could get worse than being left on the airplane, isn't it?"

Concerned with the project at hand, Lance walked into his office at Heavenly Hawaiian Honeymoon and sat at his desk.

Ron, the staff photographer, the one who had gone with him to see Hannah and her husband that afternoon, followed Lance into his office. "I've seen her with him a couple of times around the grounds."

"That's funny, when I see her he's never around." Lance commented. Instinct told him that something strange was going on. "We're running out of time and the boss is breathing down my neck. He wants that story in the spring issue of *Hawaiian Bride* magazine."

"The deadline's what?" Ron shrugged. "End of next week?"

"The end of *this* week." Lance punched the upcoming Friday square on the calendar. He had to get the coconut rolling. It was definite he wasn't going to get his interview soon, but he had to make some kind of progress. "Why don't you go ahead and snap some pics of them, Ron. That way we'll have something. We'll pick up the interview later."

"How am I going to catch them?" Ron shot up from his chair. "I'll tell you right now—I'm not stalking them."

"You won't have to." Lance pulled two tickets out of an envelope. "I'm going to send them to the Ohana Malihini Luau tomorrow night."

"Ah . . . Ohana Malihini." Ron smiled and nodded approvingly. "Oh, big *grind. Da lomi salmon, da kalua pig, lau lau. Brok'da mout.*"

"Yeah, they've got great food and plenty to eat. But that's not what you're there for." Lance had to point out. "You're there to take their pictures. You won't look out of place, there are plenty of people with cameras."

"Good idea, boss." Ron hoisted his camera bag onto his shoulder on his way out of Lance's office. "Don't worry, I'll get your pictures."

Hannah waited at the dolphin fountain for Christine and Tim. She didn't want to go but she had promised them. It wasn't the stars she wanted to avoid, it was Jeremy.

"I'm so glad you're here, Hannah." Christine looped her arm through Hannah's on her right side, while her husband stood on the other. "Tim really wanted you to come with us."

Hannah wondered if Tim just felt sorry for her. That would be pathetic.

"Do you think you'll be bored if you go two nights in a row?" Tim led the way following the signs that said: SEE THE STARS!

"I'm not worried about being bored," Hannah replied, then whispered to Christine, "I don't know if I can stand to see him again."

Christine nudged Hannah and pointed. "Is that him over there?"

Yes, it was. He was standing with a group of people. The telescopes were set up in same place with the same tiki torch lighting the area.

Good-looking as ever, all six foot plus of him in a pair of shorts and a tee shirt with a picture of the planet Saturn. But tonight, unlike last night, Jeremy was smiling at her.

Smiling. Then softness and a touch of sorrow reflected in his eyes when he met her gaze, like he'd known he had hurt her.

"Find the three stars of Orion's belt." Jeremy pointed into the sky for the crowd around him. "See—they're all sort of close together. Then . . . you see the reddish star on the right of it?"

The murmuring quieted and everyone agreed that they saw the red star.

"That star is Betelgeuse, Orion the Hunter's left shoulder. And about the same distance away on the other side of the belt is a bluish star. That's Rigel, Orion's right foot."

With everyone else's attention averted to finding Rigel, Jeremy glanced back at her again. She hadn't imagined it. If Hannah thought she was nervous before, she could feel her pulse double and butterflies had migrated to her stomach.

Hawaiian butterflies.

Jeremy had hoped that Hannah would show up tonight. Although he would have understood completely if she hadn't shown up, but there she stood, next to a couple who were looking through the telescope.

He started in her direction and a woman called out to him, "Doctor Jerry?"

"I'll be right with you." Jeremy stalled before moving to the far set of scopes to speak to Hannah.

Taking a few steps away from her friends, she met him halfway. Jeremy stopped, facing her, and said her name. She said his and smiled back.

He was glad to see her smile. He was glad to see her period. "I'm sorry, okay?"

She said nothing. He ran his hand down her arm and she didn't even try to pull away. Jeremy took it as a good sign.

"It's all my fault, I'm an idiot—big time. It was all a mistake. I was wrong. I've really missed you. I need to talk to you but I can't"—he glanced over his shoulder—"Not now. Will you wait until I'm finished? Come back when everyone's left?"

He wasn't sure she would say yes, and who could blame her, he'd been a jerk to her last night.

"Doctor Jerry?" the same woman called to him again.

Jeremy had to go but he wanted his answer. "Please," he implored.

Hannah felt her heart beating hard. She didn't know what to do. She thought he never wanted to see her, much less talk to her right away, tonight. *Was there hope? Could they patch their friendship?*

She could feel his eyes, pleading to her, through the dark and silence. *How could she say no?* She didn't want to say no, and she had no intention of saying no.

"Yes," she finally answered. "I'll come back, and we'll . . . talk." Or whatever.

"Great, okay . . . I'll see you later." Jeremy's smile widened and he headed off, turning back a couple times to wave and wink.

Hannah, who could feel a smile growing, strolled back to Christine and Tim. Christine hadn't taken her eyes off her for a second, and probably saw her speaking to Jeremy. Tim was totally into whatever it was he was looking at.

"You've got to see this Crab Nebula, Chrissy." Tim couldn't even move away from the telescope while he spoke. "It's too cool."

"Okay, dear, in a minute." Christine patted Tim on the shoulder and rushed over to Hannah. "What was that all about? What did he say to you?"

"I'm not sure." Hannah wasn't. "Jeremy said he'd made a mistake. That he was wrong."

"Wait a minute . . . you met a man who admitted he was wrong?"

This was not the time for jokes.

Hannah looked at the Crab Nebula after Christine and they both followed Tim to the next set of telescopes aimed at another deep space object in Orion.

Jeremy stood with a group of people not far away.

Christine glanced from Jeremy to Hannah. "Look at him, Hannah. He is totally flirting with you."

"Do you think so?" Hannah whispered to Christine. She didn't have to look to make sure, she could feel it. His gaze warmed her all over.

"Doctor Jerry, a question," a woman standing next to Christine called to him.

In a half dozen steps he was next to the woman. "I'll do my best to answer."

"What's the name of that other red star, the one you said was the bull's eye?"

"It's called Aldebaran." He pointed into the sky. "You follow the three stars of Orion's belt upward until you come to an orange-red colored star, Aldebaran."

"He's so smart." Christine was leaning over Hannah's shoulder, picking up sky watching tips. "And doesn't smart look sexy?"

Hannah looked from Aldebaran to Jeremy. Being smart was just another facet of his complex, fascinating personality. And, oh-yes, he was sexy. Not only was he smart sexy, his sexy was sexy.

The woman nodded that she saw the star. "Isn't Aldebaran the star Darth Vader blew up?"

Jeremy got a dazed look, like he'd been broadsided.

"You know, the place where Princess Leia is from?" the woman continued.

"I don't know." He replied, sounding confused. Apparently her hint didn't help. "It's been a long time since I've seen *Star Wars.*"

Hannah cringed and held her laughter inside. So much for being smart.

By 10:30 P.M. everyone had left, Luka had helped Jeremy take down the telescopes, and he waited for Hannah to return.

"I see everyone's already gone."

"Yeah, I'm glad you came back." Jeremy met her on the path. Now that she was here he didn't want her to go. "You didn't have second thoughts about it, did you?"

"Not one."

"I wasn't very nice to you last night. I'm sorry about what I said. That Taurus and Gemini crack was way out of line. I thought—"

"You thought I was married."

"Luka, the guy who showed you to your room that first day, he told me you were staying in the honeymoon suite."

"How did you find out that I wasn't married?"

Jeremy looked away, ashamed. "I overheard you talking in the dining room this afternoon."

Her and the blond. Probably the same blond she'd been with tonight.

"I didn't mean to eavesdrop, it sort of happened." Jeremy took her hand in his.

Hannah didn't know if it was hers or his hand that shook. Someone was nervous, maybe both of them. It felt so good to be near him and touch him again.

"I thought you were married and well, you aren't. And I liked being with you and . . . I've missed you. I want to spend time with you again." Jeremy glanced up from their clasped hands and met her gaze.

He meant it, every word. She could see it in his eyes. Jeremy was afraid she'd say no.

"I'd like that too." She leaned into him and he wrapped his arms around her for a hug. He didn't release her until he'd pressed a kiss on her cheek.

"I don't understand," he whispered. "Why do people think you're married and why are you in the honeymoon suite alone?"

Chapter Five

"Do you want to tell me about it?" Jeremy seemed as if he wanted to hear everything she had to say.

"*Are* you willing to listen to the whole mess, from the beginning?"

"Only if you want to tell me."

Hannah looked around. "Not here. We don't know who else is listening."

"Want to go out for a drink?" He indicated the poolside bar with a glance. "The lounge?"

"The lounge still has ears." Hannah smiled. What they needed was real privacy. "Ever see the honeymoon suite?"

He gestured her forward. "Lead on."

Hannah linked her arm in his and led him down

the path between the coconut palms toward the hotel and started her story.

"Up until last week I was engaged to marry Earl." Hesitation laced her voice. "He and I have been going together since we were sophomores in high school. He proposed to me a month after we graduated."

"You thought you were going to get married," Jeremy easily guessed.

"I thought we would eventually, but a year went by and then another and another." She shrugged. "Well, it just never happened."

"You know what they say, time flies by when you're having fun." She shrugged. "We weren't having fun and we weren't in any hurry to make wedding plans—at least Earl wasn't."

"And then Christine, she's my best friend, was getting married." Hannah glanced at Jeremy. "I was her maid of honor and we went to a bridal fair to check out dresses, cakes, flowers—"

"Doing your maid of honor duties."

"That's right, and there was a contest given by Heavenly Hawaiian Honeymoons, giving away a free two week honeymoon. She entered and I thought—what the heck—I had a fiancé."

"So you did."

"I jotted her wedding date as mine and—" Her comfort level dropped. Hannah did not enjoy telling her story.

"That's understandable." Jeremy didn't want her to feel bad, he wanted to hear what she had to say and be supportive. "You had to write something down."

"I guess I thought if I won . . . maybe Earl would go for a free honeymoon in Hawaii and we'd finally get married. But really, what were the chances I would win?"

Normally the odds were terrible, but in Hannah's case . . . well, she was here. "I assume your chance of winning was excellent."

"Who'd have thought it would happen? I didn't." And she still didn't look too happy about it. "Earl was excited at first. He said we'd fly out here, tie the knot, you know in a small island chapel or maybe on the beach . . . we'd work something out. He isn't big on planning ahead."

Jeremy guessed not. Even in Hawaii you had to have a marriage license and although he'd never checked, he might have thought it would take more than a day to acquire one.

"We made it as far as Los Angeles. He was going to run for a quick burger between flights and he told me to go ahead and board. He said he'd be right behind me. I didn't know he was going to run *away*."

Poor Hannah. Jeremy didn't want to feel sorry for her but leaving her on an airplane to take a honeymoon by herself was pretty low.

"A flight attendant handed me his note, that was written on a hamburger wrapper, just before take off."

"And you were already on your way." Jeremy finished for her.

"Thank goodness Christine was here when I landed. I really felt lost."

"What was she doing here?"

"She and her new husband Tim are honeymooning on the same island but at a different hotel."

"Maui is very popular with the newlywed set." Jeremy figured being the only single woman in the land of lovers could not have gone by unnoticed.

Jeremy looked up at the main tower looming above them. The Honeymoon Suite was waiting. It was sort of scary. Hannah led the way into the elevator, down the hall, and through the double doors of her room.

"This is first class." He whistled while he took in the spacious suite.

"Sorry about the mess." Hannah swept past him and snatched the clothing strewn around the room.

"The Earl influence?"

Hannah nodded and stashed the clothes she'd collected into the next room . . . bedroom, Jeremy figured. He walked through the decked-out living room with floor-to-ceiling windows and stepped out onto the lanai.

The sound of the ocean with the gentle island

breeze provided the perfect backdrop to the beautifully illuminated hotel grounds. Jeremy could see the waterfall in the distance and blue glow from the resort pools.

"Must be some view in the daytime. If Earl only knew what he was missing." Truth be told, Earl was missing a lot more than the first-class view. He'd lost Hannah. And Earl's loss was Jeremy's gain.

"Can I get you something to drink? Eat? I've got a basket full of fruit from the Wailea Neilani Resort and a bottle of champagne compliments of Heavenly Hawaiian Honeymoons."

The gift baskets had been sitting there for days and Hannah had felt guilty that a real honeymoon couple hadn't enjoyed them.

"I'll pass on the bubbly, but I'd be interested in slicing up the fruit for a midnight snack." Jeremy rubbed his hands together in anticipation.

Hannah headed to the kitchenette for a plate and a knife while he explored the goodies in the overflowing, ornate fruit basket.

"Here, this looks good." He handed her the papaya. "So now you're on your honeymoon in Maui without a husband. I guess that explains why you're alone in a honeymoon suite." Jeremy squeezed the mango, testing its ripeness. "Are you having fun yet?"

"I enjoy myself plenty when you're around,

maybe too much." Hannah had sliced up the papaya and passed him the plate. "I've still got to tell the contest people what happened to Earl."

"They don't know?" Jeremy choked.

"It's not as if I haven't tried. I know I can't accept the prize and I'm more than willing to pay for my flight and the room."

"I'm sure it'll all work out."

"I tried calling them when I first arrived, Sunday afternoon, but their office was closed and they didn't have an answering machine. But then Lance Dumont, he's the contest representative, came by to check up on us and. . . ."

"And you didn't explain everything to him then?" It was hard to believe she could have this much trouble when the representative showed up in person.

"I *tried* but he kept talking. He wouldn't let me get a word in and by the time he left I hadn't a chance to tell him."

"What about the next day?" Jeremy had sliced and diced the mango.

"I was going to call first thing Monday morning when they opened but—"

"I took you snorkeling Monday." Realization dawned on Jeremy's face.

"Yeah, I got distracted, but I had such a great time." Hannah smiled, remembering the first time in the ocean with Jeremy by her side.

"I did too, if it's any consolation." Jeremy's

confession was tinged with guilt, she could hear it in his voice. Hannah hoped he didn't really feel guilty, she certainly didn't blame him.

"Anyway, I tried calling them when I got back to my room but it was too late, they'd closed for the day. But I did have a message from Lance Dumont saying that he was going to stop by and see us this morning and I panicked. I did something stupid. I ran downstairs and bought—"

"A bunch of men's clothes to convince him a man lived here with you."

"I didn't expect to see you in the clothing store. I tried to hide them and I ended up feeling bad about that too."

"Did it work?"

She looked up at him. "You want to know if I fooled him or if I couldn't go through with it?"

Jeremy didn't answer, but the look on his face told Hannah that he wanted to hear it from her.

"I tried telling him the truth." Hannah didn't want Jeremy to think the worst about her, that she'd lied. "But he wouldn't listen. He's still after me to get an interview and pictures for their magazine."

"Good luck." Jeremy gestured with his slice of papaya. "It's going to be pretty hard to get pictures with you and Earl."

Hannah could only sigh. "I'd say it's pretty much impossible."

* * *

The next morning they snorkeled a good three hours before calling it quits. Hannah caught her footing on the beach and stood, straining to hold her ground as the surf tried its best to keep her in the ocean. She pulled the snorkel out of her mouth and raised her facemask, pulling it off her head.

"I could snorkel everyday." She tossed her head back and squeezed the water from her hair.

"Don't you snorkel everyday?" Jeremy teased her.

"Just about." Hannah looked over at him. Beautiful might have been the wrong word to use in describing him but it fit.

He looked like a statue come to life emerging from the sea. Beads of water clung to his leanly muscular arms and chest. If she could just bottle that smile of his and take it home with her she'd be a happy woman.

Jeremy made her feel wild, free, and exotic when he looked at her. Hannah loved being here, loved discovering her adventurous side, and loved spending time with him. How was she going to go back to a normal life in Kansas?

They returned to their lounge chairs next to the pool and set their fins, snorkels, and masks on the ground, sitting for a few minutes to rest and dry off.

"Can you believe the nerve of that turtle?" Hannah would have never in her life imagined she'd see a sea turtle swimming in its natural habitat.

"He had nothing to worry about, did you see how big he was?"

"I loved seeing those schools of bright yellow Tangs, and what was that brown roundish fish we saw with the big eyes and tiny cute mouth?"

"That was a puffer fish."

"Is that the kind that blows up like a balloon with spiky things all over its body?"

"That's it."

Amazing. Everything was amazing here. Hannah would never get used to it.

"What are we going to do for lunch?"

Jeremy stared right at her as if her face held all the answers. Except lunch was not the answer to life. "I know better than to let you try and skate by with a glass of POG and a couple pupus. We can go to the Poolside Café."

"Sorry. If I didn't have to eat we could get in a few more hours of snorkeling." Hannah would have felt worse, but next to snorkeling she loved sampling something new on the restaurant menu.

"That's all right." He smiled. "There are other things to do besides snorkel."

Hannah stared at him, waiting to hear what he had to say. Keep it clean. Jeremy had to remember he was talking to Miss Rebound and needed to keep reference to anything remotely intimate out of their conversation.

"There's the Iao Needle, an old battleground of

King Kamehameha, the drive to Hana that has hundreds of waterfalls and pools to explore, and locally, right over there" —he pointed to the left— "is Haleakala the volcano. You can camp or hike there or watch a sunrise and bike down."

Hannah sat up and looked behind him but couldn't quite see past the hotel towers. "A volcano? I thought that was just a mountain. Isn't it dangerous?"

"It's not active, at least not now."

"I thought they had active volcanoes in Hawaii."

"They do on the Big Island." Jeremy tossed his towel over his shoulder, picked up his gear, and headed for the equipment rental desk. Hannah gathered up her things and followed.

"That's where you work, right?"

Jeremy nodded. "The volcanoes are to the south. I work at the summit of snow-capped Mauna Kea."

"Snow? In Hawaii?" Hannah set her snorkel equipment on the desk next to his and waited for an employee to check them in.

"It might be hard to believe but we have sub-zero temperatures up there."

"Below freezing?" Hannah shot back incredulously. "Now you're just making me homesick." Dexter must have been under four feet of snow by now.

They started back to the hotel, walking hand in hand around the flamingo enclosure to her elevator bank, where they would part ways.

"I'll meet you at the Poolside Café in a half hour." Jeremy reminded her and pushed the button for her. "Don't forget to call Lance Dumont." He leaned toward her and kissed her on the cheek before walking toward his building.

Hannah pressed her hand to her cheek and couldn't help wishing that he had kissed her for real. She could hardly wait until he did.

The first thing Hannah did when she got to her room was put in a call to Heavenly Hawaiian Honeymoons. The honeymoon charade had gone on long enough and she was going to clear this up once and for all.

"Mr. Dumont isn't in right now. Would you care to leave a message?"

She did. "This is Hannah Roberts, the winner of the honeymoon contest. Will you tell Mr. Dumont that I'd like to see him as soon as possible. Thanks."

Hannah hung up the phone. She had tried . . . again. And there was nothing more she could do but wait. She'd better get moving if she wanted to be on time. After taking a quick shower, Hannah stepped into a colorful sundress to meet Jeremy for lunch.

*   *   *

Lance waited for Ron in the lobby bar. He nursed a ginger ale, wishing he could have something stronger. He *needed* something stronger. He worried about what kind of Honeymoon publicity he would get if his honeymooners were on the verge of divorce.

The new headline would read:

It's Over Even Before It's Started!

or

Ten Reasons Why You Shouldn't Bother Getting Married.

Hannah had been in pretty bad shape yesterday. It was no wonder she had acted nervous, her marriage must be on pretty shaky ground.

Lance didn't bother with a greeting when Ron arrived, he just wanted the low-down. "Give me the bad news."

"I don't think there is any." Ron caught the bartender's attention and ordered something cold. "Hannah and Hubby were together last night, holding hands, walking along the beach in the moonlight, looking at each other with goo-goo eyes, you know, like regular newlyweds. Then they headed up to their room."

"That's great." Lance set his glass on the bar, finally relaxing. Maybe things were going to turn out all right.

"Bright and early this morning they hit the water and just now I saw them heading to their suite. They sure looked lovey-dovey to me."

"That is good news." Now that the couple looked like they were back on track everything would be fine.

"I hope this will help things along." Lance waved an envelope with the luau tickets. The whole wedding experience could be stressful on some couples. Maybe all they needed was a little more island distraction. Maui was known for that. "All we can hope for is that our contest winners don't split up before the honeymoon is over."

Lance hated to think about it. It hadn't happened before, but there was a first time for everything.

Jeremy sat at the Poolside Café and didn't have to wait long for Hannah. Only five minutes after he'd been seated, she arrived.

"You look great." Jeremy hoped his eyes weren't bugging out of his head. Is that what white plumeria against a red background Aloha shirt with little spaghetti straps looked like wrapped around a woman? Deliciously tropical.

"Do you really like it?"

Hannah seemed pleased and did a three-sixty for him that gave him a good look at swirling fabric that tied stylishly at her right hip. "I got it at a dress shop called Sea Breeze, it's across from Island Outfitters."

She sat next to him and slid an envelope, logo side up across the table in his direction. "What do you think about this?"

The Heavenly Hawaiian Honeymoon logo stared up at him and he wondered if this was good news, trouble, or big trouble. Jeremy pulled out a pair of tickets and read them, "Ohana Malihini Luau."

If Hannah wanted his opinion on what to do with the tickets his advice would be to toss them and steer clear of that kind of tourist trap. But Jeremy knew her better than that. He knew that she would love to go.

"They were waiting for me when I got to my room." She looked at him, clearly excited to attend. "Do you want to go?"

"That sounds great!" *Had that come from him?* Jeremy would never in a million light-years have thought dinner with a bunch of tourists trying to get the Hawaiian experience at a luau as *a great time.*

But he was smiling and he felt part of him really wanted to do this. The more Jeremy thought about it, the more the idea of going to a luau with Hannah grew on him.

What gives? He couldn't figure out if he was going nuts or suffering an early midlife crisis.

"I'm so excited. I can't wait."

Her enthusiasm was one of the things he loved

about her. Jeremy thought she might forget all about lunch and shoot straight to the luau.

"Have you ever been to one?"

"No." Dare he tell her he found the whole idea ridiculous? He used to, that is. But going with Hannah was something else completely, a luau didn't sound half-bad. "What are you supposed to wear, anyway?"

"What else?" Hannah smiled. "An Aloha shirt."

Hannah couldn't understand how Jeremy could be in Hawaii, live in Hawaii, and not own an Aloha shirt.

Not a single one.

He might have known his planets but he didn't study its inhabitants.

The luau was tonight, which meant they'd have to shop right after they'd eaten lunch. And she knew men, most men, hated to shop and worse yet—hated to shop under pressure. Hannah promised to make this as painless as possible.

She'd make it one-stop shopping for Jeremy, one store and that was it. And she knew exactly where to take him.

After finishing lunch, they headed to the stores located on the lower levels of the hotel. Hannah slowed when she neared the window that held all sorts of objects carved out of all sorts of beautiful dark Koa wood.

Inside Paradise Carvings were carved tikis, totems, statues of people, animals, and fishes, boxes in various shapes, and bowls in dozens of sizes, lining the store. They even had a full-sized outrigger canoe hanging on the wall.

Fascinated, Hannah stepped in and ran her hand across the smooth surface of a large bowl before stepping toward something else that caught her eye.

"Do you have a boat at home or are you planning to use that to get back to the mainland?" Jeremy stared at her.

"It's Hawaiian wood." Hannah noticed that she held a five-foot Koa wood paddle. "No. I . . . this is so beautiful I had to . . . I don't have a boat. I'm just admiring it." She set it down and left the store before she found something she couldn't live without.

Jeremy slowed, then stopped at the window a few stores down from Paradise Carvings, next to the Island Outfitters clothing store.

"Did you see this? It's something Hawai-ian," he said sing-songy.

Hannah turned to look at him. "What is it?" She backtracked, stopping next to him. Standing side by side, she and Jeremy stared into the jewelry store window and she saw the delicious sparkle of gold.

"It's Hawaiian gold."

She leaned closer and her eyes widened as she took a good long look. The strategically placed lights reflected off the perfectly etched flowers and leaves in wide bands of gold with black enamel painted around the edges were called Heirloom Hawaiian jewelry. Hannah read it right off the sign.

Heirloom jewelry came in bracelets, necklaces, rings, and earrings. Styles varied from types of filigree and others that had engraved names filled with black enamel. She'd never seen anything like it. Beautiful.

"Is this something you need?" He teased, holding her to the spot in front of the jewelry case.

She looked from the glittering gold to Jeremy. "Maybe." Hannah hoped she wasn't drooling.

Could he see how much she liked them? It was difficult enough for her to walk away from the beautiful carved Koa boxes in Paradise Carvings, but what girl could say no to jewelry?

Not her. Just because she wanted them didn't mean she could have them. If Hannah were here on a regular vacation she might be able to get away with bringing home a Koa box, a bowl or two, and a paddle along with the earrings and a bracelet she thought would look nice dangling around her wrist. But with the situation being the way it was the souvenirs would just have to wait. She had other considerations to make.

"Since I'm going have to pay for my room and the flight, I'd better hold off until I know how my finances work out."

"I can't tempt you? Just a little?"

Hannah couldn't believe he said that. Jeremy tempted her more than he'd ever know. She hated to admit it, but if he made a move to hug her, to kiss her, to go any further, she'd probably go for it.

He waggled his eyebrows and pointedly looked at the glittering gold in the window. *Oh, he meant the jewelry, not him. How disappointing. Yeah, the jewelry was good too.*

"You're bad." Hannah slapped his shoulder, playfully. "We're here to shop for you not me. Don't try and sidetrack me. Come on."

Hannah wrestled her way out of his grasp and hauled him off to the clothing store next door.

"Just for that we're wearing matching outfits."

"Matching outfits?"

That should have sent fear shooting through Jeremy but he didn't look scared. He smiled.

Matching outfits were supposed to be a threat of the worst kind, hated and feared by men. Hannah thought it was supposed to be *all* men.

Most men, it seemed, but apparently not Jeremy.

She followed him around the store while he eyed the different displays. Jeremy walked up to a strapless purple sarong with white flowers and yellow pineapples.

"This would look great on you." He picked up the hanger and held the dress up to Hannah.

"You think so?" She looked down at herself, approving his choice, a plumeria and pineapple print.

"I wonder if we can find a shirt that matches this dress." He shuffled through the display rack, sliding hangers from the right to the left before moving to the next rack, continuing his search. "Small, medium, medium—I think I need a—"

"Large?" Hannah didn't guess as much as she confirmed what she'd already suspected.

"Yeah. Do you see one?" Jeremy stopped searching and looked at her, waiting for an indication of where the last remaining large size would be. "Where?"

Hannah flashed a guilty, embarrassed smile. "I've already bought it."

"You buy this shirt for Earl?"

"I didn't buy it for Earl." Hannah tried to ignore the warmth in her cheeks and confessed, "I bought it for you."

Chapter Six

That night at the luau, Jeremy had suggested Hannah avoid any alcoholic drinks, which turned out to be very good advice.

The man was a genius, which wasn't a shock to Hannah. Not only was it a good idea because it spared her head, forgoing the mai tais and chi-chis left room in her stomach for more food.

After watching the ritual of unearthing the kalua pig the luau feeding frenzy began. There were lots of people and long buffet lines.

Hannah tried the lomilomi salmon, fresh Mahi Mahi, and the guava chicken that turned out to be a variation on orange chicken. The rice and sweet potatoes rounded out the buffet along with various other seafood, shrimp, and crab. And she couldn't help herself but load up on her standard favorites, pineapple, papaya, guava, and mango.

"I'm glad to know you won't be stealing my pineapple, but you might want to leave some for the other guests."

"Oh, ha ha." Hannah returned. Jeremy was just picking on her again and he probably thought he was so funny. "I've left plenty of fruit."

"Is there anything you don't like?" Jeremy was probably amazed she didn't try to eat the lei they slipped over her head when they arrived.

Hannah had just stuck a finger full of purple-colored-looking peanut butter that sat in a small wooden bowl into her mouth. Tasted like . . . like . . . she wasn't sure she'd ever tasted anything like this before.

"Poi," he supplied.

She pulled her finger out of her mouth and groaned, waving her hands as if that would help get the taste out of her mouth. Hannah swallowed hard, forcing it down.

"It's an acquired taste. Most people, I should say most *haoles,* don't like it." Jeremy handed her a drink to wash it down. Judging by the look on his face, mirroring hers, she needed it. "Not everything tastes like white bread."

Hannah had told him at their first lunch together that nothing in Hawaii was what she was used to eating. Tasting all the new and exotic food in Maui was just heaven—a new adventure with every forkful.

The guests sat on grass mats at low tables adorned with long, shiny green ti leaves and bunches of exotic, fragrant flowers in a wide range of colors.

"Gotta give you credit, you were brave enough to try it. Not everyone is game to eat poi."

"Is this safe?" She pointed at what looked like a square of white gelatin. After her last trek into tasting new foods, Hannah felt a little more cautious this time.

"It's one of my favorites and I think you're going to love it. Haupia is coconut pudding." He urged her to eat up, if she had room left, he kidded, and downed his with no problem.

Jeremy looked wonderful in his purple Aloha shirt with festive print. She didn't know why he didn't have a closet full of them and wear them all the time.

The lights on the stage came up, signaling the start of the entertainment. Hula girls, traditional Hawaiian songs, Tahitian and Samoan fire dancers took turns on the stage in a two-hour extravaganza show that ended with the audience on their feet, cheering.

Hannah clapped when they sang the 1962 hit song *Tropical Mists*. "I love this song. It's one of those oldies you hear all the time."

"I don't know the words. I'm terrible at remembering lyrics, any lyrics, doesn't matter what song." Jeremy confessed and seemed content to enjoy the music.

For an encore the emcee sang, for all the honeymooners, *The Island Love Song.*

"My love of my life. . . ."

As many of the guests did after the luau, Hannah and Jeremy took a walk down the beach. Tiki torches lit the way, with the ocean on one side, sand and civilization on the other.

"I am so full," Hannah groaned.

She should have been. The only food she didn't have seconds of was the poi.

That was the best time Jeremy'd ever had at a touristy luau. Who would have thought he'd love it? And the night wasn't over.

He admired Hannah's lean, curvy figure. She was beautiful enough to run in the Miss Sandy Beach Contest. Her skin was much too pale for island living, but he'd bet that after another week of vacation she'd have a deep, healthy bronze glow.

She was definitely a knockout. Hannah's excitement for trying the new and different made her fun to be around. Jeremy would never be able to understand why Earl wouldn't marry her. How could Earl not have loved Hannah?

Jeremy didn't want to take the time now to calculate the odds, but he could assume they were high on the astronomical side.

The same blanket of stars hung above them as the night before. The same stars Jeremy had looked at hundreds, thousands of times, only now they looked . . . sparklier, brighter, and more beautiful than he remembered.

And he thought the entire change in his perception had to do with Hannah. It was amazing how one person could change another's universe. Even Jeremy had to admit the Aloha shirt was comfortable and he wouldn't mind wearing them on a regular basis.

On the flip side there was Hannah's sarong. Strapless and clinging to her like a wet leaf on a well-shaped seashell. She gave the bright yellow pineapples the illusion of tumbling with every step she took. And he could swear the white plumerias were fragrant or maybe it was just Hannah's own lovely scent.

"This is where you work, isn't it?" Hannah reached into the sky as if embracing the stars.

"In that direction, but way, way, way out there. Farther than we can see." Jeremy stepped up next to her and slid his arm around her waist, staring deep into space with her.

"What made you want to become an astronomer? Why weren't you an oceanographer or an archeologist?"

There was a loaded question. Did Hannah have enough time to hear the whole answer?

"My father and my brother are astronomers. I guess I never thought of doing anything else."

"Oh, it runs in the family, then." She stepped away from him and took hold of his hand before heading down the beach. "Are they as dedicated as you are?"

"I don't know if they're more dedicated than I am, but they started a long time before I did. They've already made their career discoveries."

Hannah stopped and stared at him. "They've discovered stuff . . . things? In space?"

"My brother has detected planets orbiting a distant star in a far-off galaxy and my father is known for his theories on dark matter."

"And you?" She gazed at him anxiously. He hoped she wasn't expecting to hear about an outer space expedition or a Mars colonization project.

"I'm what you'd call a late bloomer."

And that was putting it nicely. Jeremy had wasted a lot of time playing around while his father and his brother, Robert were already busy working.

"I'm looking for deep space colliding galaxies. I didn't get serious until a couple of years ago. I'm afraid that I won't get my shot in the limelight for another decade or two, if it ever happens."

"You mean you might never find anything?"

"Space is pretty big, and there are a lot of people looking. Most astronomers don't, not in their lifetime. They're committed and work hard exploring, searching for a new discovery, but most of the time you just work."

"They don't find anything?"

"There's lots of room and things are really spread out." Jeremy didn't want to be in that category. He was willing to put in his time and effort. Nothing worthwhile was ever easily attained.

"Look, look!" Hannah ran ahead and picked up something off the sand, a coconut that had washed ashore. She held it out, showing him.

"Aren't you full yet?" He had no idea where she'd put all that food. A hollow leg?

"I don't want to eat it, silly." She held it out for him to see. "It's cool. A real coconut."

"I got a news flash for you. The kinds of coconut you've been eating are real too. Here, let's see that." Jeremy took the coconut from her and brushed the sand off. He pulled out his pocketknife.

"What are you doing?"

"A little wishful thinking." He leaned against a tree trunk, pulled the debris off the husk, looking for the flattest surface and starting carving. "Tell me about Earl."

Hannah rolled her eyes. "You really don't want to hear about him."

"Yes, I do. I want to know all about you, and he

was a part of your life." Jeremy knew she'd lived in Kansas all her life and when she looked at the Pacific Ocean she studied it like it was an undiscovered planet.

He'd seen them all—Arctic, Indian, Atlantic, and Pacific. He'd even seen more than seven seas, but he never looked at them as she did . . . with real appreciation.

Something in Jeremy ached. There is so much she hadn't seen and at this moment he wanted to show them all to her. Hawaii alone had great variety—lush tropical greenery, desolate volcanic features, and snow-covered peaks—not to mention the prehistoric petroglyphs.

Moving on from the Hawaiian Islands, Jeremy thought of the glaciers in Alaska, mesas of the southwest, Louisiana swamps, and the everglades in Florida. Beyond the United States there was even more. There was so much for her to see in the rest of the world.

"You really want to hear about Earl?" Hannah moved to a hibiscus bush and picked a large red flower.

"Yeah. Tell me, will you?" No, he wasn't weird. Jeremy just wanted to know everything about her—warts, meaning Earl, and all.

"Hmm . . . where do I start?"

He could see her mentally wrestle with herself, trying to find a good starting point.

"Well, I didn't have a mom and dad. They died in a car accident when I was twelve. I grew up with my aunt and when I got to high school I met Earl. He was there, always there. I guess I sort of thought I was in love with him. Right now I can't even tell you why."

Jeremy blew off the loose husk shavings and turned the coconut and continued carving.

"I didn't expect to be swept off my feet by being serenaded or to be showered with rose petals. All I wanted was to be loved. As far back as I can remember I'd always loved Earl. I've always wanted to marry him. And I thought he loved me too. I suppose I was wrong."

"I can't believe what an idiot he was not marrying you." Jeremy would be the last one who'd understand the guy.

"I guess he didn't enjoy being engaged to me so he must have figured marrying me wouldn't be any better. I didn't expect all that much from him, really. He wasn't the kind of guy that would fulfill a woman's secret fantasy or anything."

"What kind of fantasy?" Jeremy looked up from the coconut. *Would she tell him?* Asking about fantasies was getting personal, but he really wanted to know. "I grew up with a brother . . . I haven't a clue what women think."

"I think every girl has romantic dreams about her wedding day." Hannah got that far away look on her face. "Wearing the long, flowing white wedding dress, seeing the perfect man wait for her at the end of the long walk."

In the next moment she shook the dreaminess away and shrugged. "But they get over it and realize that stuff like that isn't real and only happens in the movies. I guess that's all over now. He's probably back in Dexter going about his business."

"What are you going to do when you go home?"

"I don't know. I guess it's pretty clear that we're not going to end up together. If I were really smart I'd move out of the state. I don't think I could live in the same place, the same city, anymore."

Jeremy was listening to her, but every time he gazed into Hannah's eyes he got lost and tended to zone out. He really should pay attention to what he was doing. He was working on an uneven surface with a sharp blade.

His heart pounded, maybe it was the excitement over the haupia, maybe he'd had too much poi, what Jeremy knew for sure was he hadn't had enough Hannah.

"You know, this wasn't the way it was supposed to be. I thought we were going to get married and . . ." Hannah glanced over at Jeremy, who had momentarily stopped carving and hung on her every word.

"Aw, forget it." Hannah stepped away from him and stared out toward the ocean. The waves on the beach were illuminated with light from the luau nearby. "I was a stupid teenager who believed in true love and wanted the house with the white picket fence."

"The white picket fence is not a bad dream . . . just not realistic nowadays . . . it's more like a small condo in the suburbs." He readjusted the coconut and stared at it intently, resuming his carving.

"I'd have settled for that, too, but I didn't know that Earl wasn't going to stick around. It took Christine and Tim getting married for me to realize that he really wasn't interested in me."

"You have time, you're still young."

She looked from the ocean over her shoulder at him. "Are you going to tell me not to worry because I have my health? That would be sad."

"You have youth, health, and beauty, and a guy can't help but be crazy about you." Jeremy handed the coconut to her.

Hannah read: *H. R. + J. G.*

She glanced up at him, flashing a shy, approving smile with the tilt of her head.

"It'll be our secret." Jeremy took the coconut from her, readying to send it on its way. "Want to wish it luck?"

Hannah kissed her fingertips and pressed them to the initials.

"Now to make the wish come true." He took the

coconut from her and stepped back and threw it as far as he could out over the ocean. The coconut disappeared into the darkness and out of sight. With the surf splashing in front of them, they didn't even hear it land.

"Won't the waves just bring it to shore again?" Hannah stepped back until she stood against him.

"Eventually, when it comes back, someone will see it and then it won't be a secret anymore." Jeremy ran his hand over her bare shoulder. Her skin felt smooth, warm, sexy. He slipped his arms around her, holding her near.

Hannah smiled sweetly at him and he knew his coconut carvings had touched her. "Did I tell you how handsome you look in your new island wear?"

Jeremy could feel the warmth of her hand as she slid it up his shirt. He wished the shirt wasn't there. He wished she'd just slide her hand under the material. He wished. . . .

"I don't know why you never wore an Aloha shirt before, they're so exotic."

Maybe not exactly exotic but they weren't as bad as Jeremy had thought either.

"You look like every man's tropical vision." He took the red hibiscus flower and tucked it behind Hannah's left ear.

"Isn't wearing a flower behind one side mean you're available and the other means you're taken? Do you know which is which?"

"I think there is some kind of rule like that, but I don't know what it is." Jeremy slipped his arms around her, holding her near, and she felt very, very good. "We could compromise and. . . ."

He had to be careful. Hannah was on the rebound and she was probably vulnerable. The last thing he wanted to do was hurt her. One little kiss couldn't hurt, could it?

"If wearing a flower behind your left ear means you're available, then I'll take you, and if it means you're taken, you'll be mine."

He wanted to kiss her. One little rebound kiss shouldn't hurt either one of them. He knew his limits. Jeremy would never, ever take advantage of her.

Just one little. . . .

He leaned close and looked into her eyes before bending down and meeting her lips.

"What are you doing?" she murmured with her eyes were still shut.

"Kissing you. Do you want me to stop?" Maybe he shouldn't have. Maybe she wasn't ready for this, for him.

"Maybe . . . in a minute." Hannah opened her eyes and wrapped her arms around his neck to pull him near for a second kiss. "I'll let you know."

Hannah and Jeremy both glanced to the left when they saw the flash of light. He didn't know what it was, and he really didn't care. Maybe it was a tiki torch flare-up or a meteor fragment hitting off-shore. All that mattered was he had Hannah in his arms and he didn't want to stop kissing her.

Jeremy couldn't stop himself from wrapping his arms around her and pulling her tight against him. It might have been too soon for her, but for him it was too late.

Chapter Seven

"Who is this guy?" Lance Dumont stared at the man in the purple Aloha shirt with the white flowers and yellow pineapples. It was one of the pictures Ron had taken of Hannah and her husband from the luau—the luau that she was supposed to attend with her *husband* . . . not some stranger.

"It's *Mister* Henderson, isn't it?" Ron swung around the desk to stand at Lance's side and get a better look.

"No—yeah, no . . . I don't know . . . it's supposed to be but—" Lance pulled the Henderson file out from his stack of folders and flipped it open, shuffling through the paper for their picture.

It was here somewhere.

Lance pulled out the color, 5-by-7 picture from the folder and carefully studied the man in it before comparing him to the gentleman in the luau photo next to Hannah.

The woman in both pictures was Hannah, but the man—Lance looked from one photo to the other again. The two men were not the same. And Lance was dead sure that an Aloha shirt did not change facial features.

The man named Earl Henderson had a longer, thinner face with straight, light hair. The man at the luau was broader, more muscular looking, with darker hair. They didn't even look close to being the same person.

Lance couldn't believe this. He took a second look at the picture from last night. *What the heck was going on?*

If Earl Henderson hadn't gone to the luau with Hannah then who was this guy? And what had Hannah done with her husband?

Another morning of snorkeling gave way to another afternoon lunch. Jeremy was convinced that Hannah could do this every day for the rest of her life and never tire of it.

On the other hand, he knew how much more of the world there was to see and as sad as she would be leaving the Hawaiian Islands, Jeremy was positive Hannah would love to see what the rest of the world had to offer.

The phone rang just as he had finished putting on a pair of shorts and a red and orange Aloha shirt with large, white hibiscus. He wouldn't have been caught dead in this before but with Hannah around, he was changing his mind about island wear. Jeremy found that he was changing his mind about a lot of things these days.

He picked up the receiver and the instant before he said, "Hello." He wondered, and perhaps wished, that it were Hannah calling to tell him that she missed him so much she had to hear his voice.

Oh, brother. When did he start getting sappy about love, relationships, and life?

"Jerr, how you doing?" It was Russell.

"Hey, Russ. Doing fine."

"So how's it feel? You having a good time over there? You feel the need to celebrate?" There was a smugness Jeremy couldn't identify in Russell's voice.

"This amateur astronomy stuff is not as bad as I thought. It's sort of like a mini-vacation and yeah, I'm having fun." He wouldn't have minded at all about extending his stay for another week, especially since Hannah was here.

"That's not what I'm talking about. What does it feel like to have discovered a comet?"

"A comet?" Jeremy had to sit and he settled onto the bed. *Had he heard right? He'd discovered something?*

"You know that fuzzy area you had me check out near Orion? It's a comet . . . I guess now it'll be known as the Gordon Comet."

Jeremy had discovered a comet. He thought there'd be some private jazz band celebrating inside his head when the moment happened, but it hadn't. He didn't feel like he'd discovered anything of importance. He felt . . . nothing.

"It was then near the star Eta Orion, near the border of Taurus and Eridanus. Do you know how rare visual discoveries are?"

"It was a mistake. I was looking for the M42 and started from the wrong star and. . . ." Somehow he thought making a discovery would be more profound, more earth shattering than it had been.

Jeremy had thought that having something named after him would feel like he'd done something, make him feel more important. It hadn't. Having the Gordon name attached to it sounded the same as if his father or brother had made the discovery, not him.

"It's not a done deal yet. You're going to have to confirm readings, get the numbers and—you know the routine—so we can have it verified."

That meant Jeremy had to get his hands on some equipment to make his claim.

"With my fast talk and immeasurable charming ways I've managed to steal you some scope time on Maxwell," Russell bragged. "If we're lucky we can get a real good look at it, download some data to analyze later."

If Russell really managed to find time on a big telescope he was *The Man*. Jeremy would have to share the credit and insist the comet be renamed to the Gordon-Yamada Comet to acknowledge his colleague's contribution.

"You're gonna owe Kaminski big time for this." There was the sound of shuffling papers before Russell continued. "You're up first on Saturday and they'll only give you a couple hours. I know it's not much time, but you shouldn't need much time since you know exactly where to look."

So the bottom line was that he had a flight out of Maui at 9 A.M. on Saturday. Jeremy had to get to the airport, fly to the Big Island, and get his rear over to the observatory so he could set up for his bartered scope time to make his discovery.

His discovery. Jeremy smiled, he liked the sound of that.

Jeremy was floating on air as he walked through the hotel lobby. He could hardly believe it—he'd discovered a comet!

He could almost sing a song and dance a jig on his way to meet Hannah in the Grand Dining

Room, but he couldn't remember any words to any comet songs, and decided to give up on dancing a comet dance. Hopping around doing the comet dance without music would make him look like a dope.

Everything was working out for him. He had his comet and his girl. Life was wonderful.

He wondered how excited Hannah would be. He couldn't wait to tell her, to share it with her. But then it dawned on him that running off on Saturday to make his discovery meant running away from Hannah, leaving her. And he didn't like the way that sounded.

Jeremy's feet became heavy, and once again, he was earth-bound. Having the comet to look forward to didn't make leaving Hannah any easier. The real problem was he didn't want to leave her.

Thinking about Hannah reading the news in the paper wasn't the way he wanted her to find out what he was doing. Having her in a different state or even a different country wasn't his idea of the wonderful life he thought he had just seconds ago.

Jeremy wanted to tell her, he wanted her to be there with him. He wanted to show her all the places he'd been. With Hannah he'd experience them like he had never seen them before, with an enthusiasm, an excitement that he hadn't had the first time around.

Off to the left he saw the glimmer of gold calling to him—the gold from the Nani Pono Maui window. A soft voice somewhere inside told him that years from now the Hawaiian gold piece would remind Hannah of when they first met.

Years from now? Where had that come from?

Inside . . . your heart.

And he had to admit it, he loved her.

Jeremy loved Hannah.

He wanted her to go with him, be with him, tomorrow, the day after, and the day after that. He wanted her to go with him after Hawaii—to Peru, Italy, Australia, where ever.

He wanted them to be together . . . for always and forever. Jeremy wanted to marry her.

Marry her . . . what a great idea.

Why hadn't he thought of this sooner? Sometimes he was so dumb.

Yes, oh yes!

If he bought a ring now, tonight would be the perfect time to pop the question. He thought about how Hannah would react, how surprised, and hopefully delighted, she'd be.

Yes, yes, yes . . . he'd do it.

Stepping inside the jewelry store, Jeremy looked at the different styles of rings. No traditional diamond solitaire for her. With Hannah, he'd go completely native.

Jeremy narrowed his choices to the Hawaiian jewelry that she'd once admired. There were barrel or domed-etched bands that were decorated in black enamel, scalloped tropical flowers, and carved leaves.

Which would she choose?

He decided on the filigreed plumeria band, edged with black enamel. Jeremy made sure that if she wasn't happy with his choice that she could bring it back and get the ring she wanted.

The weight of the ring box in his pocket was a constant reminder of this big plan. It was all he could do not to pop the question that afternoon, but he wanted to wait. Wait for the perfect moment.

He had to, for Hannah's sake. Earl may not have thought about what marriage meant to her, but Jeremy had. He wanted to create a romantic memory and had hoped that it would come close to fulfilling one of her fantasies.

Tonight, after he'd finished with his lecture and answering the guests' questions, he and Hannah would walk down the beach as they had the nights before. It would be a lousy night for stargazing, but it would be a perfect night for romance.

It would be exceptionally beautiful with the moon at its fullest, shining down on the ocean. He'd suggest they lay in one of those rope hammocks and listen to the waves whispering to the sand and drawing new secrets out to the sea.

Jeremy was going to ask Hannah to marry him, and for the present time, he was the only one who knew, but it wouldn't be for long. He'd ask Hannah, and she'd be wearing his ring, and she would make him the happiest man in the universe.

He couldn't wait to see how different things would be for them in just a few, short hours—and how happy they were going to be.

"Lance . . ." Josephine came in with a handful of papers. "I was just going over our travel accounts and this one. . . . This is just so strange, but there was an airline ticket refund and reissued, and the airlines charged us for reissuing the ticket."

"Refund? And reissued to where?" That's all he needed now was another problem popping up.

"I don't know."

"Well, find out," Lance snapped. The pressure to complete the magazine layout was growing. With the discovery of Hannah's mystery man, the situation wasn't getting any easier. He didn't need an added complication of wayward airline tickets. This honeymoon contest was turning into a who-done-it, featuring him as the lead detective.

"Okay," she replied, but the look on her face said she didn't appreciate him taking out his frustration on her.

Lance and Ron made it through the stack of proofs taken at last night's luau. Lance was no closer to finding out what was going on than he had been a couple of hours ago. He'd called and left a message for Hannah to call him back as soon as possible. It was nearly noon, was she with that same man now?

A half-hour later, Josephine stepped in again. "Got it." She read from a sheet of paper. "Earl Henderson turned in his ticket in Los Angeles and booked a flight back to Wichita, Kansas last Sunday."

"Last Sunday?" Lance felt his blood pressure jump a couple notches. Last Sunday was four days ago and he was only finding out about it now?

If Earl Henderson hadn't been here all this week and Hannah had—Why hadn't she told him?

Lance let out his breath and thought about the times he'd seen her. She'd always been alone, once he'd caught her red-eyed and crying.

She had wanted to tell him something, he re-membered. Lance never found out what it was. He'd just assumed it was bad news he didn't want to hear.

"I want to talk to Earl Henderson right now." Lance must have sounded mighty fierce because Josephine raced out of his office to make it happen.

Finally, Lance was going to get to the bottom of whatever was going on.

Jeremy was all smiles when he finally showed up for lunch. He pressed a loving kiss on Hannah's cheek before taking a seat next to her at the table.

There was something different about him. Not as obvious as the way he smiled or acted. It was something small and slight in the way he looked at her, like he had a secret.

"Have you heard back from Lance Dumont yet?" Jeremy straightened out the utensils and took a sip of water. Then Hannah noticed his gaze never left her eyes.

"I called again and they said he would be in touch. That's it. But I haven't heard a peep from him since."

Jeremy had something to tell her, she knew he did. And it was starting to make her feel a little nervous and anxious.

"And you?" she encouraged. "What's going on? It's something exciting, I can tell."

"Russell from the observatory called me," he began calmly. Hannah sensed that his insides were bubbling.

"And?" She leaned forward.

"And . . . well, a few days ago I'd called him and asked him to check out a fuzzy spot I'd spotted close to Orion."

"Yes, and?"

"He checked it out and . . ." Jeremy smiled, making her wait even longer. He was doing it on purpose, the rat. Could he tell how much he was torturing her?

"Did he find something?" She paused. "What

did he see?" She waited a little longer. "Come on, Jeremy." Hannah hoped he wasn't going to make her stand and stomp her foot and demand that he tell her right here, right now.

He looked away and back to her again. "Aren't you hungry? Would you like to order lunch first?"

"No, I want you to tell me what Russell found. He saw something, didn't he?"

"Did he?" He repeated, teasing her. Jeremy was enjoying every second of her suffering.

"Jerr-ee-mey." She groaned impatiently.

"Russell said there's a comet there."

"A comet?" She blinked, taking it in. "That zings through the sky with a long tail that comes around the Earth every so many years?"

"*My* comet." Jeremy said it as if he could hardly believe it himself. "I've found a comet."

"Oh, my gosh! That's so amazing!" Hannah felt like she was in the presence of a genius. She'd never known anyone who'd done anything of global importance before. "Is it coming this way? Will we be able to see it? You know, us—the people on Earth? Will it come back again and again like Halley's Comet?"

Jeremy held up his hand, trying to squelch her questions, or was it her enthusiasm, maybe he just wanted her to be quiet. Hannah couldn't help it, this was exciting news.

"I don't really know anything about it yet." Now the modest, bashful scientist appeared.

"When do you find out? How will you find out? What do you have to do?"

"On Saturday after I—" he stopped and the smile fell from his face.

The mood between them suddenly became somber, but she could have easily finished his sentence for him. "You mean, after you leave."

"This doesn't have to be the end for us, you know." He didn't sound very optimistic. "It's not as if we'll never see each other again. We can still—"

"I don't want to talk about your leaving now."

It was too sad to dwell on. Hannah wanted to enjoy the day, revel in Jeremy's discovery. She wanted him to have fun—*she* wanted to have a good time because their time together was limited.

"I don't even want to think about it." Hannah closed her eyes, willing herself to keep positive. "We have another whole day together and I just don't want to spoil it with sad thoughts."

"Okay. We'll talk about it . . . later." Jeremy reached across the table and held her hand. "There will be a later for us." He said it as if he were certain.

Hannah wished things could be that easy. She wished she knew what was going to happen. Life was complicated—her life was anyway. She had to straighten out a lot—the mess with Lance Dumont, her ex-fiancé Earl, before dealing with the person she wanted to be with the most—Jeremy.

She wouldn't get depressed about this, she promised herself. Meeting him was one of the best things that had ever happened to her. She'd had a great week, he'd been the best eye-opening experience of her life.

And she couldn't say what she was afraid to admit to herself—she loved Jeremy, plain and simple.

She loved him.

Hannah wasn't going to nurse a broken heart after they parted. She'd be happy because he was happy. He'd gotten what he wanted—a discovery.

But she couldn't help wondering if he felt the same about her as she did for him. They'd had such a great time together, the whole week while he was here—and maybe, to him, that's all it was.

Just because they didn't talk about tomorrow being their last day together didn't mean they weren't thinking about it. The rest of lunch was a real downer. Even though Jeremy knew what was coming, if he had said anything to indicate anything different he might have ruined tonight's proposal surprise. So he kept his mouth shut.

*   *   *

"We're going to have to cut this short tonight," Jeremy announced to the guests. "The moon will be out and its light will wash out some of the stars." What it really meant was the stars were in his favor.

Jeremy followed the regular schedule, pointing out the planet Jupiter, Taurus the Bull, and Orion the Hunter. The rising moon made the nebulas and the Pleiades pretty much impossible to see.

But the evening was tinged with sadness. Hannah smiled at him every now and again, but that was only when she caught him looking at her.

Only after everyone had left and the equipment had been put away did the evening really begin. Jeremy patted his pocket, making sure he still had the ring before taking her for a short stroll down the moonlit beach to the empty hammock strung between the coconut trees. The time and place were right and Jeremy was finally alone with Hannah.

Hannah's vacation was only half over, she had another week on the island paradise. But what kind of a paradise would it be without Jeremy? Come tomorrow he would leave. And what was she going to do without him?

Who would be her swim buddy and tell her the names of the fish? Who would give her a bad time about how much she ate? Who would she kiss goodnight?

Jeremy helped her recline into the hammock

and settled beside her. Cuddled up next to him, Hannah felt safe and warm, and she knew it was a false sense of security.

She didn't need a knight in shining armor on a white horse to save her, what Hannah needed was a genie in a bottle with three wishes.

"Did you see that?" Jeremy pointed straight ahead into the night sky.

"See what?"

"A falling star." It figured that the astronomer in Jeremy might be more interested in what was happening above them than between them.

Another shot across the sky followed by a second and a third, and she saw those. Hannah could feel the muscles in his arm holding her snug against him. Did he get his strong arms from wrestling with those telescopes?

"A meteor or two isn't unusual but there isn't supposed to be a shower tonight," he announced, sounding like a news reporter.

She preferred to look at him than any meteor shower or listen to any 24-hour news service. His eyes were warm and expressive, his nose strong and masculine. His smile exhibited his personality. It was the tiniest bit crooked and rose higher on the right.

"Maybe it's magic," he whispered.

What did he say? Did the logical thinking

astronomer—scientist just call lights in the sky magic?

Jeremy met Hannah's gaze and gave her that adorable, slightly crooked smile she cherished. *Was he talking to her?*

He ignored the falling stars, stroked her cheek with his thumb, and leaned toward her for a kiss.

It was like a dream . . . and Hannah was ready, had been ready to kiss him. Jeremy made her feel all tingly and alive, complete.

Kissing had never felt like this, never. It felt as if they were floating, in more than just the hammock, off the ground. Her insides were melting—in a good way.

She relaxed, catching her breath.

"You're right," as she ran her hand down his chest, smoothing his shirt and staring into his eyes, "this is magic."

Hannah leaned toward him again, wanting to make fireworks of her own, but then stopped when she saw . . . or she thought she saw someone . . . him . . . here?

But it couldn't be.

"Earl?" Hannah pushed herself up and out of the hammock, nearly flipping Jeremy onto the ground. "Earl, is that you?"

Chapter Eight

"Hey, babe. Surprised to see me?" The thin guy wearing a T-shirt saying, *This tee shirt would look good on your bedroom floor* and a dark blue baseball hat headed straight for Hannah. "I'm back and ready to do you right."

"What are you doing here?" She moved out of his reach when he neared. *This was Earl?* Jeremy swung out of the hammock and landed on his feet, wanting a better look at the guy. The guy Hannah *used* to love. Looking at Hannah now, Jeremy didn't know what to think, her expression was unreadable.

"Hey, dude," Earl mumbled to Jeremy in what he guessed was supposed to be a greeting.

A second man approached, ignoring Jeremy completely. "Surprise—Hannah Roberts!"

"This is my buddy, Lance." Earl clapped the man on the back. "He's the one who's come to our rescue."

So this was Lance Dumont. Jeremy focused on the man who had brought Hannah almost as much grief as Earl had.

"It took us a while but we now have the whole story about you two." Dumont stood between Hannah and Earl as if he were physically trying to bridge their gap.

Jeremy knew what Hannah's side was, he wondered what "story" Earl would have told. *Maybe Hannah had told him to get lost? Threw him off the plane?*

"We're expanding our usual contest spread." Dumont swept the sky with the new headline. *"The Hawaiian Dream Wedding—From Beginning to End!"*

Earl snapped up her hand and held it close. "I am so sorry, babe."

Hannah pulled away and tried to inch back from him. She still had a hard time believing Earl was here, standing right in front of her.

"When I got home I realized what a mistake I made leaving you. You'll forgive me, right?"

Hannah stared at him.

"Come on, I want you to marry me." Earl wore

a smile and Jeremy wondered if it was real. "I mean it."

Hannah looked from Earl to Dumont and smiled. Hers was tentative and uncertain. They had caught her off guard and blown Jeremy out of the water.

"What do you say?" Dumont sounded hopeful. "It's all up to you."

Jeremy slipped away unnoticed and found the path to the hotel to head back. He didn't have to wait for Hannah's answer, he already knew what it was. Hannah had always wanted to marry Earl, and now she could.

Hannah might have been smiling, but it wasn't because she was pleased. She couldn't believe what was happening. This was all a joke, it had to be.

"An all-expense-paid, top-notch Hawaiian wedding just for the two of you." Lance Dumont might have thought he was tempting her, but he was wrong. "And we'll extend your honeymoon another week."

The heavenly dream Hannah was sharing with Jeremy a minute ago was turning disturbingly nightmarish, and she couldn't wake herself.

"I realized breaking up before you married must have been traumatic, but I'm very happy I could have a hand in getting you two back together."

Earl *had* come back to her. But just because

he'd returned didn't mean they were back together. And just because he wanted to marry her
didn't mean she wanted to marry him.

A tiny part inside her might have been glad to
see him again. And maybe another part that was
especially pleased to know that he wanted her.
Earl had flown all the way from Kansas to throw
himself at her feet and beg for her forgiveness.

But was it enough?

Hannah wanted to kick him while he groveled,
but she managed to restrain herself.

Earl tried several times, until he succeeded, to
slip his arm around her. She had no doubt Lance
Dumont thought that a full reconciliation would
be near. Why? Because Earl came back and
wanted her? But Hannah had news for them
both—it wasn't going to be that easy.

She wasn't sure what she was feeling. Flattered,
confused, and angry . . . all of it overwhelming,
Hannah found this too much to take in. She didn't
know what to do and she just let it all *happen*
around her.

"Just picture it"—Lance went on and set the
stage for her—"A wedding at sunset, right on
the beach. Red, orange, and pink rays shooting
from the horizon, lending a multicolored backdrop
to your special day. Doesn't that sound romantic?"

"Sounds great, babe, doesn't it." Earl's uncertain gaze roamed to her. They wanted her final

okay but she wasn't going to give it. She wasn't going to say anything.

"You can be married in the chapel on the resort grounds if you'd like."

Hannah wasn't sure if she liked any of those choices, especially if they included Earl.

"You can be in a traditional or modern-day tropical Hawaiian dress—of your choosing, of course. Anything you want." Lance held his arms open, making it seem as if he were offering her the world.

It was hard to tell who could stoop lower—Earl or Lance Dumont. His desperation came through loud and clear.

"We'll have fresh flowers, dozens of different kinds of orchids—dendrobium, paphiopedilums, cattleyas, and photographers to capture the moment."

"I don't know. I can't think about any of this now." She struggled away from Earl and stepped back from the two men standing in the moonlight by the empty hammock.

Lance continued. "That's okay, you sleep on it. You have all day tomorrow with the wedding consultant to make your plans for Saturday."

Yes. No. Hannah didn't know what to think, everything was happening so fast.

"Listen, now. Let's not make any rash decisions, shall we?" He stepped in between Hannah and Earl, drawing them closer to his sides. He was trying to will a spark to ignite between them.

Hannah wasn't sure if there ever could be; she wasn't even sure if there ever was one. She must not have looked convinced of Earl's affection because Lance kept working on her.

"He loves you, Hannah, and I know you love him. I can see how he might have hurt you, but I can assure you that he's ready to step up to the altar."

Was there nothing this guy wouldn't do for a story? Hannah decided no, he'd probably do almost anything to get what he wanted.

"Hey, buddy." Lance clapped Earl on the shoulder and pulled him to one side. "Why don't you go to the bar over by the pool and get us some drinks—a couple of beers for us and a mai tai for your lady. Just tell them I'll be right there to take care of the tab."

"You'll pick up the tab?" Earl smiled and nodded, with his *I-win* victory body language. "Sure thing." He ambled off, leaving Hannah with Lance.

He waited until Earl was out of earshot before continuing. "You know, I don't believe in the saying, 'bad publicity is better than no publicity at all.'"

"What is that supposed to mean?" A feeling of uneasiness washed over Hannah.

There was a change in his demeanor. The once brown-nosing, I'm-willing-to-bend-over-backwards for you attitude turned sinister, threatening.

"That means I'd much rather be involved with a lovely newlywed spread than a criminal fraud suit."

"A criminal. . . ." *He wouldn't really press any charges, would he?*

"Let's not mince words here." Lance stepped closer to her and looked her directly in the eyes.

Gone was the congenial, enthusiastic representative from the Honeymoon sponsor. In front of Hannah stood the decisive, self-possessed man who would do what he had to in order to get what he wanted.

"You won the contest stating you two were married and accepted an all-expense-paid honeymoon. In accepting that prize you gave us rights to an exclusive story and pictures to be used for promotional purposes."

Hannah had no doubt that he meant business.

"Number one, you've accepted the prize by flying out here and occupying the honeymoon suite for the last week. And number two, you're not even married. This sounds like fraud to me."

Sounded like blackmail to Hannah.

"You were in love with Earl, you probably still love him," he said in an overly understanding tone and a devilish smile. Hannah doubted he understood anything. "You're just angry with him right now. What you need to do is take some time, cool off, and think it over—really think it over. Carefully."

Hannah was numb. She didn't know what to think, but threats were certainly not going to help make up her mind.

"I'm sure you'll make the right decision." He looked off into the dark.

A few seconds later, Earl appeared, returning with the drinks and handed a beer bottle to Lance and a tall stemmed glass decorated with a little festive paper umbrella and a slice of pineapple to Hannah.

"Here you go, guy."

"May I propose a toast?" Lance raised his beer bottle and Earl followed. "To the happy couple."

Hannah hung up after phoning Christine and stood there, resting her hand on the receiver. Her hometown friend wasn't Hannah's first choice.

She wanted to call Jeremy. Hannah wanted to talk to him, to find out where and when he had disappeared. She wanted to know what he thought about what had happened. She wanted, just wanted, to hear his voice.

But calling him would be a mistake. Inside she knew that she and Jeremy were over, and whatever they might have had would never be. He didn't want to hear from her—ever.

"Who were you talking to, babe?"

Hannah pulled her hand away from the telephone and took two steps back, like she'd been caught cheating or something. What she was really feeling guilty about were her not-so-platonic thoughts of another man.

"I was calling Christine but she wasn't there so I left a message." That had been the truth, she had called and left her best friend a message.

"I thought Chrissie was on her honeymoon. Where did she go again?"

"Maui." Hannah had told him at least a dozen times before they'd left Kansas last week. If he'd paid any attention to what she'd said, he'd know Christine and Tim were honeymooning on the same island they were on.

"Oh, yeah, I remember."

That was a lie. Hannah knew he hadn't.

"What's with all this fruit?" Earl rummaged around the kitchenette, plunking some papayas, mangos, and a whole pineapple on the counter. "Aren't there any chips here? Oh—here we go." He tore the bag open and left the fruit where it lay.

Hannah didn't want to tell him he was diving into a bag of, not potato, but taro chips, which would have made him spit. She was certain he couldn't be bothered to read the label and find out what he was really eating.

"By the way," he said between munches. "Who was that guy you were with in that slingy-thing?"

"Oh, he was . . ." Hannah didn't exactly know

how to explain Jeremy. "He and I were . . ." And why did she have to tell Earl about Jeremy? "Well, I met him that first night when I . . ."

Earl snorted and sat on the sofa, putting his feet up on the coffee table, crossing them at the ankles. "Never mind, it doesn't matter. I don't really care."

Earl didn't care? He was supposed to marry her and he didn't even care that she was hammocking with another man?

"This is a great room. I can't believe you stayed here all by yourself." Earl patted the sofa seat next to him. "Weren't you lonely?"

"No." She sat on the other end of the other sofa as far as she could away from him.

"Not even once?" He didn't sound like he believed her. Earl sounded like he was trying to be playful, cute.

Earl didn't do cute very well.

"No. Not even once." She couldn't tell him that she had Jeremy. *Had* was the right word and the right tense—as in past. Jeremy was out of her life now.

"Hey, babe." Earl set down his beer bottle, got up from the sofa, and moved nearer to Hannah, inching his way over to her. "You and me in this big room—we can get into all sorts of trouble, what do you say?"

Hannah felt a little self-conscious being alone

with Earl. It wasn't the same as it had been before. Before he left her, before they were going to get married, before she'd met Jeremy.

"We could—" He puckered his lips and made smooching sounds, kissing the air.

"I don't think it's a good idea." She scooted away from him.

"It's a great idea. How about some—" He ran his hand up and down her arm, which was putting her in the mood, but probably not the mood Earl wanted. "And maybe we could—"He waggled his eyebrows and motioned to the bedroom with a jerk of his head. "You know, huh? What do you say?"

I don't think so.

"We shouldn't have to wait, right? We'll be married in a couple of days anyway, so what does it matter?"

It did matter. Hannah stood up. She wasn't going to be forced into anything she wasn't ready for or didn't want to do.

But would she risk going to prison instead of marrying Earl?

"Forget it. We're not married and I'm sleeping in this room, in that bed alone. You can sleep out on the beach for all I care."

"Okay. I get your point." Earl glanced around. "Where's my bag, then? I'll hightail it to my own room."

"Your bag?" Hannah marched to the bedroom to get away from him. She wished he'd just high-tail it out of her sight. Where he went, she really didn't care.

"Do you keep it in your bedroom next to the bed so you can keep me close?"

"You want to know where your bag is? Check with King Neptune," she told him and slammed the door.

"King Neptune? Is he the king of Hawaii?"

Hannah switched the phone receiver from her left ear to her right. She knew full well that Christine was really going to give it to her royally when she heard the whole story.

"I got your message and all I can say is—I can't believe it. You're getting married? Isn't it a little soon?" Christine lectured Hannah early the next morning. "Jeremy might be a great guy but marrying him is a little rash, don't you think?"

"Not Jeremy, Christine." She was so glad they weren't in the same room when she told her best friend. Hannah really didn't want to see the expression on her face or hear her scream. "I'm supposed to be marrying Earl."

"Earl?"

There was silence.

Dead silence. For a long, long time.

Hannah wasn't sure how long it stretched out, but it felt like hours.

"Christine, please?" Hannah bit her lower lip, hoping she wasn't about to lose her best friend, and the only shoulder she had to lean on.

"Are you telling me that you're going to marry that deadbeat who abandoned you on the airplane on the way here?"

That about said it all.

"Can you honestly tell me that after everything he's done to you that you still want to marry him?" Christine was really getting heated up over this.

"This isn't about wanting to marry him. It's about being blackmailed."

"Blackmailed?" Christine gasped. "Who? Why?"

"It's Lance Dumont over a magazine story."

"He wouldn't send you to jail, not really."

"I think, yes, really. He's serious." Hannah took a deep breath and told her, "I'm supposed to make the wedding plans today for a sunset ceremony tomorrow." She begged her. "I need you." And she beseeched. "*Please.*"

"Oh, Hannah." The anguish in Christine's voice made Hannah feel worse than she already did. "Don't move. Just don't do anything—I'll be right there."

Hannah could not imagine Christine's frantic

state of mind on her twenty-minute walk from her hotel to Hannah's suite.

"Hello, you must be Christine, Hannah's bridesmaid. I'm Helen Nihei, the resort's wedding consultant. Please come in." She pulled the door open, allowing Christine in.

"I think we should get started right away." Helen gestured for Christine to take a seat on the sofa next to Hannah. "There are lots of decisions to make today so we can get started with the preparations for tomorrow. We want everything to be perfect, don't we?"

Christine sent Hannah a look that told her they needed to talk. Privately.

"Can I get you two any refreshments before we start?" Helen glanced from Hannah to Christine. "We've got a lot to go over, dresses, flowers, music, cake, and decorations all this afternoon."

"Can I get something to drink, please? Fruit juice, Guava?" Christine spoke first.

"That sounds great. Guava juice for me, too," Hannah added. "Thanks, Helen."

"I'll just step into the bedroom and call room service and be back in a minute." Helen disappeared into the bedroom, leaving Hannah and Christine alone.

Christine stared at Hannah in disbelief. Face to face, there was no way Hannah could hide her feelings from her best friend. "So you've made up your mind. You're really going through with this, aren't you?"

That had been the plan. Hannah wasn't sure it was her plan. Everyone around her was moving in that direction. And she didn't know how she could stop it.

"I don't see that I have a choice, Christine." Hannah thought she was going to cry. She didn't know what she was going to do. "I'm so confused. I know Earl came back to me and I was mad at him, but then I realized that life without him wasn't as bad as I thought so—"

"Wasn't bad?" Christine glanced skyward and leaned back on the sofa. "I've never seen you happier than when you were with Jeremy."

"It doesn't matter. I'm never going to see him again." There, she said it . . . out loud. She hadn't wanted to admit it was true. It was over.

Is that what the problem was? She didn't want to go home after a wonderful vacation? Is that what she thought of Jeremy? Earl represented the real world and Jeremy was a vacation?

"I don't know what to do, Christine." And she didn't. "I just don't know anymore."

"Whatever you decide"—Christine touched Hannah's arm, lending strength—"I'll be there for you."

Hannah gazed through tear-filled eyes at Christine, then stared out the window into the distance. The blue, blue of the sky touched the aqua blue of the ocean, meeting in a discernable line, forming the horizon.

As much as she would have liked to sit and stare at that beautiful sight forever, she couldn't. Real life was intruding and she had to face the music—and it sounded a lot like *The Wedding March.*

Helen emerged from the bedroom. "Room service is on their way. Come on, ladies, let's get started, we have a Hawaiian wedding to plan."

Whatever Hannah had or might have had with Jeremy was gone with him. Earl was here and ready to marry her. She had loved him for a long time, but she felt differently about him. She didn't even think of Earl in the same way.

Hannah had grown up.

"Let's begin with the legal details. The marriage license agent will be arriving at four P.M. to meet with you and Earl. No blood test is required and there's no waiting period."

Hannah's heart raced, not even the state of Hawaii put up any barriers to delay her wedding. She still hadn't made a decision: marry Earl or face fraud charges.

"As far as the ceremony, I'm told you've chosen a non-denominational service. I should tell you that there will be a little added Hawaiian flair, so if you prefer a strictly civil ceremony you need to let us know."

Who was Hannah to say no? When in Maui. . . .

"Next, you need to pick out a dress. The seamstress will be here in"—Helen glanced at her watch—"fifteen minutes to take your measurements."

Retrieving a photo album, she set it on the coffee table, opening it for Hannah and Christine.

"I'd recommend since you're getting married on the beach that you wear a casual dress, sleeveless, perhaps strapless in three-quarter, tea, or ankle length." Helen flipped through her photo album, showing an example of each style to Hannah and Christine. "The traditional Hawaiian bridal wear is called a *holoku.*"

Hannah stared at the picture of a long-sleeved, loose, seamed, fitted dress with a yoke, and a train.

"Here's a non-yoked variation worn slightly off the shoulder, without a train." Helen turned the page and pointed to a beautiful tailored dress. "This is the one. That's the one I would recommend since you have a beach ceremony. They're usually made out of white cotton, satin, or silk."

"Sounds fine to me," Hannah agreed. It was beautiful, of course she'd love to wear it, but she wondered if all these plans were ever going to materialize into a real wedding.

"Fine?" Helen sounded a little confused. "This is your wedding, you should be excited to pick out your dress. If there's some other style you'd like— Please, feel free to make your own choice."

"No, the *holoku* is beautiful. I'm just feeling a little numb. I only found out I was getting married yesterday and my mind is . . ."

"She'll be fine, really." Christine came to Hannah's defense and wrapped a comforting arm around her.

"Shall we go on?"

"Please." Hannah put on her best smile and tried to act more positive.

"Would you like a bridal veil or the *haku* lei?" Helen pointed out a bride in one of the photos. "A *haku* is a woven garland of island flowers worn on your head. We can match the *haku* flowers to your bridal bouquet if you like."

Flowers weren't a hard decision. Hawaii was full of every kind imaginable and orchids were plentiful. Hannah and Christine had chosen flowers in white and pale lavender and yellow.

"After the ceremony the chapel bells will ring in celebration and you'll move to one of the gazebos in the chapel gardens for wedding cake and a champagne toast."

Wedding cake . . . Hannah wondered if *haupia* was the traditional flavor. The decision made her feel

weepy. She knew she'd love it and so would someone else, but she wasn't marrying *someone else.*

Haupia or not haupia?

If this hadn't been her and Earl's wedding this
wouldn't have been a big question. Earl was a
plain chocolate and vanilla man, and before coming to Maui Hannah would have been too. But in
the last week Hannah's tastes had changed in cake
and, she had to admit, in men.

Chapter Nine

It was Hannah's last night as a single woman. This time it was for real. She'd been happy about it the first time around, but she was far from pleased this time.

Lance Dumont had taken care of everything and made dinner reservations for her and Earl at the Island Reef, a romantic open-air restaurant with its outdoor Polynesian-themed atmosphere.

Hannah and Earl were seated in a secluded spot, outside on the very edge of the terrace. Must have been the best table in the place, she guessed. The cascading waterfalls, meandering streams, and lush foliage didn't improve her dinner date.

Maybe Earl's charm had worn off on her. Hannah was more apt to believe that he never had any charm.

"The Catch of the Day is Mahi Mahi," the waiter announced. "Our fresh fish today are Ahi, Ono, Opakapaka, and Opah. You can have our chef prepare any fish for you baked, broiled, grilled, sautéed in an island seasoned butter, or breaded in Macadamia nuts or Panko and fried lightly in olive oil."

"Is fish all you have?" Earl grumbled. "Don't you have burgers?"

Seafood was the main attraction in Hawaii, Hannah had learned that much in her week's stay. Earl didn't care for fish at any time, fresh or not.

"We serve Island burgers." The waiter pointed to the item in Earl's menu with his pen.

No one bothered to say it was from the Keiki's menu, and Earl didn't ask.

"Okay, I'll have one of those, without the pineapple. I don't want fruit touching my meat."

"Island burger with pineapple on the side." The waiter suggested.

"Make that on a whole separate dish."

"On a . . . separate . . . dish," the waiter repeated and wrote in his notebook. His raised eyebrows probably went unnoticed by Earl. "Fine, sir. And for the young lady?" He looked up at Hannah.

"I'd like the Mahi Mahi grilled, please." Hannah handed her menu to the waiter. "Iced tea to drink."

"And you, sir? A beverage for you?"

"I'll have a beer."

"A beer." The waiter glanced up from his pad. "Will there be anything else?"

"I don't think so, thank you." Hannah replied before Earl had a chance to throw in a *nope.*

Earl opened the drink menu and scanned the pictures. "What did you order?"

"Ugly fish," Hannah whispered, to herself, re-membering her conversation with Jeremy that first day after they snorkeled. She smiled at the memory, it seemed so long ago. It seemed like a dream or a whole different life. Someone else's.

"What did you say?" Earl strained to hear. "Fish? Ugly fish? Since when do you eat fish? I don't care what it looks like, I'm not eating fish." He stuck his nose in the dessert menu that had been sitting on the table, reading it like the number one choice on the *New York Times* best seller's list.

This was supposed to be romantic—the dinner, the setting, and the atmosphere. It could have been, it might have been, but it could not have felt more wrong.

Hannah sat back in her chair and instead of gazing into Earl's eyes, she stared out and up into the sky. Last night she had been with Jeremy, only twenty-four little hours ago, and she was having the time of her life, literally. That all came to an end when Earl had showed up and changed everything.

She'd wanted tonight to be special, not special because of Earl's arrival, but special because it was supposed to be her last night with Jeremy. Before he went back to work on the Big Island.

Now she was back to real life, burgers, beer, and Earl. How did this ever happen? Hannah glanced at Earl then back into the darkening sky.

She never knew how much of the world she was missing until she met Jeremy. And there was more out there, but life with Earl would keep those experiences undiscovered.

Jeremy was leaving tomorrow. Nothing would change that. She wouldn't even have a chance to say good-bye or thank you. Hannah would never forget him.

The hotel grounds' lights washed out all but the larger stars' light, which included a line of three which Hannah recognized as Orion's belt.

The illuminated pool area in the distance left only the two single bright stars on either side of Orion's belt—Betelgeuse and Rigel—visible.

Orion was the last constellation Jeremy talked about during his sky watching lecture, and tonight would be the last time he'd give that lecture.

How she wished she were there.

Taking a deep breath and letting it out slowly, she wouldn't cry in front of Earl. He'd just get mad. He'd never understand about her *sniveling* over another guy.

Knowing they shared the same sky should have been some comfort to Hannah but it wasn't. Jeremy might as well have been on Jupiter, he felt so very far away.

Hannah stared at Rigel, the blue, brighter of the two stars and blinked back her tears, wondering if he would look at the same star, the same constellation, and think of her.

Jeremy focused the last eyepiece on M21 and a wave of melancholy fell on him. Tonight was his last night as resident astronomer and his last night at the resort.

Things hadn't turned out exactly the way he'd planned. Tonight was supposed to be their first night of the rest of their lives.

Their lives *together*.

He loved her. He thought he loved her . . . he wasn't sure anymore. But his heart was sure aching like it was broken.

How could Jeremy have loved someone who could so easily dismiss him? Earl had showed up and Jeremy never heard another word from Hannah. How much more did he need to know?

They'd been together almost every day for the last week. He would have thought . . . he should have known better, figured it out, but he hadn't.

She hadn't loved him as he loved her. He wasn't even sure what she felt about him. It didn't matter anymore. It was best for both of them that he leave.

Jeremy would never see Hannah again. Tomorrow he'd head back to work at Keck and she'd be here with Earl.

On *their* honeymoon.

Even though she'd be only an island over from him, it would feel like she was halfway across the earth, maybe in another star system.

The moon's glaring light washed out all but the brightest stars in the sky. Betelgeuse and Rigel were still bright and he could still make out Orion's belt.

Jeremy remembered that first night when she spotted Jupiter's moons, her astonishment at seeing her first nebula, and the thrill when she could distinguish between the blue luminescence of Rigel and reddish tint of Betelgeuse. She had been surprised but he wasn't.

The sad part about the way things turned out was that there wouldn't be a single night that passed when he looked into the sky and not think of her.

Jeremy could just imagine, perhaps wishfully, that sometimes when she gazed up at Orion she'd remember him too.

*   *   *

It was just Jeremy's luck that Russell, and not someone else, met him at the Kona airport early the next afternoon. They had driven to their quarters for a quick stop, dropping off his luggage, and picking up gear for the night.

The trip from the airport to the observatory would take hours. Jeremy needed to get up there to calibrate the telescope before sunset, when the observatory doors opened.

"Come on, we've got to get going." Russell left, heading for the car. "It's a good thing you came back. I might have filed for discovery first."

"So your name goes in front of mine, big deal. We both know who told who it was there." Jeremy was right behind him when his phone rang. "Just a sec," he called to Russell. The smallest, tiniest spark of hope wished it was Hannah, but that was ridiculous. "Hello?"

"Jerry-man, I call all over to find you. *Wat doing?*" Luka screamed over the phone.

"Luka?" Jeremy couldn't imagine why he was calling and how he had even found him at this observatory. "I'm at work, that's what I'm doing. Why are you calling?"

"Your girl, she marry that *haloe.*"

It wasn't a surprise to him. Jeremy knew Hannah was marrying Earl. That's why he was especially glad he'd left the resort. He knew he wasn't wanted. Where he had thought the distance between Maui and Hawaii too far away last night, right now it felt much too close.

"That's Hannah's business, not mine. That *haloe* is the guy she wants to marry."

"You *tink*? What you do?"

"I'm going to let her marry the man she wants." It hurt Jeremy to admit it. He'd never said it out loud and thank goodness he never heard Hannah say those words. It might have killed him.

"Jerr," Russell called to him. "We need to get going."

"In a minute," Jeremy answered and said into the phone, "I've got to go."

"*Da's junk. Nuff* already, you gotta come back."

"No, I'm not going back to Maui, I'm not stopping the wedding." He was not going to do it. They each had what they wanted. Hannah had Earl and he had his comet. They were both going to be happy.

"They marry when *da* sun go down." Luka threw in. "*Bodda* you?"

"Doesn't bother me at all. I'm happy for them."

Hannah loved watching the sun go down and he had no doubt she'd love a sunset wedding. Jeremy didn't want to think about how much he would have liked to share that with her.

"*Dere* on *da* beach."

"It'll be very romantic." She loved the beach, the water, and the fish. It was the perfect choice for her. Jeremy had to work hard to prevent the image of Hannah from taking shape in his mind. "I wish her all the best."

"You stop her, yeah? *Geev'um! Wikiwiki,* Piilani Highway *choke* cars. *Den* you make *beef.*"

"I don't have to worry about the traffic. I'm not going to Maui and I'm not stopping the wedding." Jeremy couldn't, it was her choice to marry Earl, not his. "And you can forget about me fighting him."

"*Aznuts.* You know what? You *lolo, brah.*"

"No, trying to stop her would be crazy. I've got to get going. I've got work to do." Jeremy hung up.

Jeremy drove the SUV south.

He'd drive south for a while until he got to the fork in the road. Left at the fork led to the observatories, going right would lead to the airport. But Jeremy wasn't going that way. He was heading up the mountain.

It didn't thrill him that he had Russell as a passenger, but his co-worker had helped him with the initial identification. Jeremy was not about to deny his colleague the official discovery.

Russell talked a mile a minute, obviously excited about the evening ahead. He talked almost as much as Hannah had when she got going.

Hannah.

How long would it be until Jeremy stopped thinking about her? A week? A month? Forever?

He didn't need to hear from Luka that she was getting married. He knew that or could have guessed.

Jeremy couldn't save Hannah. She wanted to marry Earl. But maybe. . . . Maybe if she'd had a choice—Earl or him—maybe she'd choose him.

Maybe she would.

Forget it. It's what he wanted, not what she wanted or even wished.

No, there wasn't any decision to make. He was going to the observatory. He was going to turn left—he told himself—left.

Left.

Jeremy slammed on the brakes and skidded across the oncoming lane stopping on the opposite shoulder. Russell shot forward, thankfully the seatbelt kept him from shooting through the front windshield.

"What are you doing?" Russell shifted back into his seat and caught his breath.

Jeremy shifted into first, cranked the wheel, and took off in the opposite direction.

"Where are you going?" Russell braced himself with both hands on the dashboard. "This'll take us back to the airport."

"Yeah, I know." Jeremy glanced out the window

at the traffic and pulled onto the road. Turning right, he continued on 190 south—to the airport.

"What do you think you're doing?"

"The right thing," and under his breath Jeremy whispered to himself, "I hope."

Hannah may have looked beautiful but she'd never felt worse. It took more than mere clothes to make a woman happy—this woman anyway.

She couldn't have wished for more beautiful flowers or a dress. The traditional white wedding *holoku* she wore made her feel like a princess, a Hawaiian princess, and the white ginger and lavender colored dendrobium orchids and plumerias in her bouquet and *haku* gave off the most heavenly scent, better than any bottled perfume.

"It's time to go." Helen flitted around Hannah, making sure she hadn't left anything behind. "We're going to take the elevator down to the main floor and walk out the back of the hotel toward the wedding chapel."

The words *wedding chapel* made Hannah's stomach do flip-flops.

Music from the lobby—a local island band—drifted in the background, making Hannah feel like she was in the middle of some glamorous movie. The hotel guests smiled and waved, wishing Hannah good luck. She needed it.

It was her day.

Oh, yes. Her *big* day.

Her wedding day. It should have been a glorious day. But Hannah wasn't feeling glorious, not even close. And she doubted if she ever would.

Hannah walked out the back of the hotel and paused at the dolphin statue in the fountain. The sun was nearing the horizon, getting ready to throw its magnificent light show.

The wedding chapel sat on a small rise off to the north. Photographers snapped her picture, asked her to pose, smile, look to the left, then to the right.

"Gentlemen, please," Helen interrupted. "The bride will be posing for pictures at the chapel momentarily. You can wait for us there."

Hannah and Christine were soon herded to the chapel and Helen took over, instructing them how and where to pose for the photographers.

Stand by the ferns, by the gazebo, by the chapel. . . . Hold the bouquet higher, tilt it forward, put the flowers to the side and stand without them—move to the right, to the left . . . Get the ocean in the background, get Molokini in the background. . . .

Hannah didn't like posing for pictures. She had to stand still. And standing still gave her time to think, and she didn't want to think about what was going to happen.

She'd gone back and forth about marrying Earl,

but Lance Dumont had made it perfectly clear that he would have his story. Whether the story was about a couple walking down the aisle toward happily ever after or about the jail-bound bride was her choice.

Helen stayed behind to prepare for the cake and champagne celebration after the ceremony. Christine, her maid of honor, walked beside Hannah from the chapel until they came to the beach.

A half dozen or so photographers followed her down to the sand, snapping her picture with every step, every apprehensive step. But the closer Hannah got to the wedding ceremony itself, the stronger her doubts grew. This was more than just butterflies or cold feet.

A conch shell sounded announcing Hannah's arrival and the start of the ceremony. Twenty feet away, Earl stood in a white shirt and slacks with the traditional red sash around his waist, and a long lei made from dark green leaves.

Earl smiled, he looked happy. It was the same expression as the I-got-a-free-beer happy.

The minister, clutching a small book, stood next to him, wearing a sedate-colored Aloha shirt and dark kukui nut lei.

Off to her left side, Hannah heard the auto-advance whirring of cameras. Behind the photographers stood Lance Dumont, wearing a big smile, who must have been pleased as punch. Hannah didn't know if he was really happy for them or not, but he was getting what he wanted.

Was this what she really wanted? Was Hannah really going through with this?

Clutching a white and lavender orchid nosegay, Christine, dressed in her lavender *holoku,* strolled down the beach first. Reaching the groom and minister, she stepped aside and stood with her husband Tim.

It was Hannah's turn next. She glanced around before stepping forward. With the exception of the wedding party and the photographers, there was no one in sight.

That was too bad.

Was no one going to stop her? Or the wedding? Were they hiding someplace? Were they going to wait until the part where they were supposed to object to the couple being married?

She wished they wouldn't. Don't wait. She wanted them to speak out now.

But no one came. It was her turn to walk down the beach and she couldn't put it off any longer. She kicked off her sandals, preparing to take the wedding walk, down the beach toward the water's edge.

Hannah drew in a deep breath, swallowed hard, and stepped forward. The sand was warm beneath her feet with the first few steps she took. Stepping on the ocean-dampened sand, she followed Christine's path until she reached Earl's side.

The minister smiled at her then Earl, asked them both to face him, and the ceremony began. "*Aloha Nui Loa,* welcome to you and your friends that have come together at this beautiful place to celebrate your marriage—"

Hannah glanced from the minister to Christine to Tim then back to Earl. It was happening. She was marrying Earl.

Now.

Right now.

"—a very special day that you have chosen to affirm your love for one another with spoken words, with sharing of vows, and giving of rings."

Jeremy heard a conch shell horn sounding in the distance and ran from the front of the Wailea Neilani through the lobby toward the beach. He stopped at the dolphin sculptures at the outdoor pond and glanced to the right then to the left.

Luka said the wedding was taking place on the beach and there was a lot of beach. Where should he start looking? Which way should he go?

Someone waved at him off to the right, calling his name. Luka. Jeremy took the chapel path, running past the gazebo where a woman stood next to a bottle of champagne chilling in a silver ice bucket and a small two-tiered wedding cake.

Hannah's wedding cake.

Feeling more anxious by the second, he had to

get there, find her, and stop the wedding. He sprinted around the back of the wedding chapel where he just caught sight of Luka. Luka stood behind a coconut tree and motioned for Jeremy to do the same.

Jeremy leaned against the tree trunk, trying to catch his breath before peering around it. Toward the shore, stood a minister, two witnesses, along with the bride and groom.

Hannah wore an off-the-shoulder white dress, a lei of light white, yellow, and purple orchids circled her head, matching the bouquet she carried.

She looked more beautiful than he could ever have imagined . . . ethereal.

Adornments of maile leaf lei and a red sash wrapped around the groom's waist with the traditional long-sleeved white shirt and pants even made Earl look good.

The ceremony had already begun.

"Earl and Hannah, we come here today to affirm your love for one another by celebrating your marriage. You have come individually and to make a commitment—"

Jeremy didn't think the minister meant that they had taken separate flights to Maui, a week apart.

"—From this day you will walk together as husband and wife." The minister paused. "Although our vows are spoken in a matter of minutes, they are promises you will make to one another that will last a lifetime.

"Let us take a moment to be aware of all the beauty around us, taking in a breath of air, and listening to the sounds of nature, as the waves come up on the shore and the gentle breeze caresses our faces."

Now that he was here, hearing the words of the wedding ceremony, Jeremy wasn't sure stopping it was right anymore. Is this what Hannah wanted?

"You must realize that marriage is a promise, made in the hearts of two people who love each other, and this will take a lifetime to fulfill."

Jeremy sagged against the coconut tree and closed his eyes. There was no shutting his ears to the minister's words.

"Earl, do you find within you a special love for Hannah that convinces you that you want to spend the rest of your lives together? Do you find within you the courage to face the challenges that you may encounter along your journey together?

"Earl, do you wish for Hannah to be known as your wife? If so, please say, 'I do.'"

Jeremy should not have come. This was wrong.

"I do."

Of course Hannah loved Earl. She wouldn't be marrying him if she didn't.

"Hannah, do you find within you a special love

for Earl that convinces you that you want to spend the rest of your lives together? Do you find within you the courage to face the challenges that you may encounter along your journey together?"

Hearing Hannah speak her vows to another man would tear Jeremy apart. Was he crazy?

He retreated back to the hotel lobby and back to where he belonged, Keck.

Chapter Ten

"Hannah," the Minister continued. "Do you wish for Earl to be known as your husband? If so, please say, 'I do.'"

For the rest of her life? Hannah looked from the Minister to Earl. Wondering. Thinking.

No, she wasn't sure. Could she go though with this?

The surf surged onto the beach, washing over Hannah's feet, barely touching the hem of her dress.

Under his white groom's shirt, Hannah saw an orange neckline of a T-shirt. If she looked close enough, she could see the words: *So Many Women, So Little Time* across his chest.

She strained a little harder and noticed that two

171

steps closer to him and she would have been able to see quite clearly that he hadn't bothered to shave for his own wedding.

This was so wrong.

How could she have thought she ever wanted to marry him?

She didn't want anything to do with Earl.

Hannah didn't need anyone to object to her marriage. She didn't need anyone to step in and stop the ceremony, Hannah was going to do it herself.

No matter how many arrangements had been made, no matter what the cost, no matter what the consequence, Hannah was not going to marry Earl.

The minister cleared his throat and straightened before asking again, "Do you Hannah, take Earl as your lawful husband?"

Smiling Earl stared at her. Hannah looked from him to Lance Dumont who stared back in wide-eyed expectation. She was on the spot, everyone was watching, waiting to hear what she had to say.

Hannah looked back at Earl, and it hit her— getting married wasn't the end of the world.

"No, I don't think so."

"You're supposed to say yes," the Minister prompted in a whisper. "You *want* to be his wife."

"*No,* I don't," Hannah clarified. She wanted to make it perfectly clear. She looked hard at Earl, making sure that was what she'd meant.

It was.

Turning to Lance Dumont, she said, "I don't care what charges you're going to press. It can't be worse than if I marry Earl. If I marry him"—she pointed at Earl—"it's going to be a life sentence with no parole."

"You're guilty of fraud and in breach of contract." Lance Dumont leveled his finger at her.

"I'm sorry," she repeated. "I can't do it . . . can't. Nothing you can say will make me."

Earl's smile had disappeared. He wore the miserable, everyone's-got-something-against-me expression.

Not everyone, just Hannah.

Something knocked against Hannah's ankle and she looked down. A rock-like object bobbed in the water, lapping at their feet.

No, not a rock but a coconut.

Deep lines etched in its husk looked deliberate, carvings of some sort.

Hannah picked up the coconut and read:

J.G. + H.R.

If there ever was a sign, this was it. It was like a symbolic piece of Jeremy rescuing her, telling her she was doing the right thing.

Hannah smiled and retrieved the secret message that wasn't a secret anymore. Wiping the sand from the husk, she took a second look, tracing the etched letters with her finger.

She never, ever dreamt she would see this coconut again. Tears stung at her eyes.

"You're more interested in that damned fruit
than you are in marrying me," Earl complained.

"I'm not doing this." Hannah repeated for Earl.
As she knew, he needed important facts repeated,
he just didn't seem to remember.

Christine's "All right!" punctuated the air.

Hannah handed Earl her bouquet, hung on to
the coconut, and headed back to the hotel.

"You're going to be sorry," he shouted at her.
"I'm not going to ask you again."

That suited Hannah just fine.

She wasn't getting married, but at least it was
her life now. Her mistakes, anything she wanted to
do, Hannah would decide.

She may not have Jeremy, but he had opened
her eyes, shown her a taste of what adventures life
held for her. He was right, there was more to life
than white bread or Earl and she was going to find
out for herself.

"Hey, *brah!* Jerry-man." Jeremy heard Luka
shouting over the din of daily business, the guests,
and the five-piece band playing Hawaiian background music in one of the hotel's lobbies.
"Wait—you stay."

"Stay? What for?"

"The *wahine*, she's no marry that *haole*."

Well, of course Hannah is marrying Earl. That is—Hannah and Earl were the *wahine* and *haole* Luka was talking about. Jeremy had seen them standing at the surf's edge and heard the vows for himself.

"Your girl, she *talk stink* to that *haole*-boy. She come here—now."

"Hannah didn't marry Earl?"

"Yeah, you some *akademe*, you know *dat*?" Luka smiled. "She come here, now."

"Now?" Jeremy didn't have to stop the wedding, Hannah had. And if Hannah was available, he wanted her. The question was did she want him?

He never needed to sweep a woman off her feet but he wanted to do it now. What should he do? How would he do it? A million decisions to make and a million more details to plan and all in under thirty seconds.

"Luka, come with me. I've got an idea." Jeremy grabbed a decorative basket from a nearby potted plant with one hand and dragged Luka behind him. "This is what I want you to do."

Hannah came marching through the lobby in her wedding dress, swiping at the tears on her face while clutching a sand-covered coconut. Everyone around her knew what she had just done, she just knew it. Everyone.

How embarrassing for her . . . but she didn't

care. Her life would have been far worse if she'd gone through with the wedding.

"Hannah Roberts, this is for you," a voice announced over a loudspeaker system, coming from . . . she looked around, hearing her name echo around the room.

Where was the voice coming from? Who was talking to her?

Was it Lance Dumont? It didn't matter, she was not going back. Not even if he threatened her over a loudspeaker, announcing to the whole world what she'd done. She would not marry Earl.

It was only then she realized that the entire lobby hadn't quieted. They had already been at a standstill even before her arrival.

A strum of a guitar and the trill of piano keys began and someone, a voice, a man's voice, slowly sang.

My love—of my life—

Hannah recognized it as the *Island Love Song.* The voice sounded familiar but she couldn't match it to a face. It wasn't Eric Mo, that was for sure.

I don't know what words I'm singing—for you, I've bought a wedding ring-ing-ing.

Whoever he was could carry a tune and had the melody down, but the words were all wrong. He wasn't singing the right lyrics, but he was pretty good about making up new ones.

Until this moment—I had no idea—that you left

Earl—at the altar—And I really don't care if he falters.

She wiped at her tears and headed to where she thought the music came from—the stage across from the Grand Dining Room.

Hannah gasped and had to blink a couple times to make sure she wasn't seeing things. On the stage, among the band members, was Jeremy with microphone in hand. He was crooning a tune he barely knew and making up words for the lyrics he, by his own admission, could never remember.

I have stage fear—can you come close now—near. My love for you will leave—ne-ver, you can stay with me for-ever—

Hannah squeezed her eyes closed and covered her mouth when she realized that Jeremy was singing to her—in front of all these people.

His gaze never left her, and he motioned to her in accordance to the words of the song.

His made-up words were cute, meaningful, and they touched her heart. They must have been his words because they certainly weren't the words that went with the song.

Didn't we have fun? I'm not the one to run.

She cradled the coconut closer, holding it tight while Jeremy serenaded her. Her cheeks warmed with embarrassment. Hannah still found it hard to believe that he was really singing . . . to her.

No one had ever sung to her before, it made her feel very special.

Good-byes will not be fi-nal—if you marry me to-day. I love you—

I do—

The band members echoed, making Jeremy jump and look behind him. He behaved as if he hadn't known they were there.

I do—

Hannah smelled flowers—then she noticed flower petals, raining down on her. They were falling from above, all around her in all different colors.

Then the echo sang,

I do—

She glanced around, thinking that the petals couldn't just be falling on her. But it was true. The petals were floating down on her alone.

Hannah looked up toward the balcony and spotted Luka hanging over the edge with a basket in hand. His grin went from ear to ear and he waved.

Jeremy finished up the last line of the song.

Love you—

The hotel guests applauded. Jeremy looked at Hannah and smiled. There was no doubt he'd meant this performance for her. To his adoring fans in the audience, he bowed and bowed and bowed.

When he had finished he held out his hand to Hannah. The crowd cheered when she took hold of his hand and he stepped off the stage onto the flower petals that littered the main floor below.

Hannah slipped into his arms, held on to him as tight as she could, and kissed him.

She loved him. Hannah really loved him and now she knew he loved her too.

"You really are bad at remembering lyrics." The growing lump in Hannah's throat made it difficult to get the words out.

"It doesn't matter, you're inspiration enough for me." Jeremy loosened his hold but wouldn't release her from the circle of his arms.

"What are you doing here?" Hannah ran her hand over his hair, touching him. Anything to keep him close and to touch him. "How did you know . . . that I was getting married? That I didn't marry Earl? That I'd left him?"

"It doesn't matter." Jeremy kissed her neck, her face. "I'm just glad you didn't marry that guy."

"I couldn't . . . because of you," she confessed. It was never clearer to her than now that she was marrying the wrong man. "And this."

Recognition lit his face when she turned the coconut so he could see the initials he'd carved. "Where'd you get that?"

"It's fate, giving me the thumbs up."

"Destiny," he whispered. "I spent all my time staring into outer space. I'm an idiot 'cause what I really wanted, what's really important was right here on earth."

"*Miss* Roberts—" Lance Dumont interrupted, in Hannah's opinion at the worst possible time. "Expect to hear from the company's lawyers."

"Lawyers?" Jeremy caught Lance by the arm, stopping him. "Wait a minute, pal. I thought you were here for a story."

"Story?" Lance chuckled. "There's no story here."

"Oh . . . I think there is." Jeremy smiled. "You wanted a story of love at first sight? The perfect couple and how they found happily ever after?"

Lance Dumont stared at Jeremy through narrowed eyes. "What did you have in mind?"

"Well, stick around then because we're not finished." He turned back to Hannah.

"Hannah, I love you. I want you to marry me. Will you marry me?" Jeremy pulled her into his arms, making his proposal difficult to even think about. "Wait . . . just—one—wait." He dug into his pocket and pulled out a small box. Opening the lid, he held the Hawaiian gold ring for her to see. "Say yes. Please, say yes."

"What about your comet?" It had occurred to Hannah that maybe he was doing this to save her from prison. It was very nice of him but she'd rather marry him because he loved her.

Could Jeremy really love her?

"It doesn't matter. The universe is full of them. There's only one you." Jeremy smiled, took her in his arms, and kissed her.

He didn't want to save her from prison, he wanted her for himself. How could she have thought otherwise?

Jeremy really loved her.

"Is the minister still willing to perform a wedding, Mr. Dumont?" Hannah peered over her shoulder at the Heavenly Hawaiian Honeymoon representative.

"What are we waiting for? We've got a wedding to shoot!" Lance Dumont waved the couple to the beach. His grin went from one ear to the other. "Let's do it!"

Epilogue

H AWAIIAN BRIDE MAGAZINE
SPRING ISSUE
"True Love Conquers All!"

Hannah Roberts from Dexter, Kansas and Jeremy Gordon recently of Waimea, Kona, Hawaii were united in a surprise marriage at the Wailea Neilani Resort on the island of Maui.

The couple plan to roam the world, following Jeremy's work. The first stop for the couple is Canberra, Australia. His latest discovery, the Yamada-Gordon Comet, will make its appearance in our solar system in the year 2021.